PENGUIN BOOKS

La Symphonie Pastorale and *Isabelle*

André Paul Guillaume Gide was born in Paris on 22 November 1869. His father, who died when he was eleven, was Professor of Law at the Sorbonne. An only child, Gide had an irregular and lonely upbringing and was educated in a Protestant secondary school in Paris and privately. He became devoted to literature and music, began his literary career as an essayist, and then went on to poetry, biography, fiction, drama, criticism, reminiscence and translation. By 1917 he had emerged as a prophet to French youth and his unorthodox views were a source of endless debate and attack. In 1947 he was awarded the Nobel Prize for Literature and in 1948, as a distinguished foreigner, was given an honorary degree at Oxford. He married his cousin in 1895; he died in Paris in 1951 at the age of eighty-one.

Among Gide's best-known works in England are *Strait is the Gate* (*La Porte étroite*), the first novel he wrote, which was published in France in 1909; *La Symphonie pastorale*, 1919; *The Immoralist* (*L'Immoraliste*), 1902; *The Counterfeiters* (*Les Faux-Monnayeurs*) published in 1926; and the famous *Journals* covering his life from 1889 to 1949 and published originally in four volumes.

E. M. Forster said of him: 'The humanist has four leading characteristics – curiosity, a free mind, belief in good taste, and a belief in the human race – and all four are present in Gide ... the humanist of our age.'

ANDRÉ GIDE

LA SYMPHONIE PASTORALE

AND

ISABELLE

TRANSLATED BY
Dorothy Bussy

PENGUIN BOOKS

PENGUIN BOOKS

Published by the Penguin Group
Penguin Books Ltd, 27 Wrights Lane, London w8 5tz, England
Penguin Putnam Inc., 375 Hudson Street, New York, New York 10014, USA
Penguin Books Australia Ltd, Ringwood, Victoria, Australia
Penguin Books Canada Ltd, 10 Alcorn Avenue, Toronto, Ontario, Canada m4v 3b2
Penguin Books India (P) Ltd, 11, Community Centre, Panchsheel Park, New Delhi – 110 017, India
Penguin Books (NZ) Ltd, Private Bag 102902, NSMC, Auckland, New Zealand
Penguin Books (South Africa) (Pty) Ltd, 5 Watkins Street, Denver Ext 4, Johannesburg 2094, South Africa

Penguin Books Ltd, Registered Offices: Harmondsworth, Middlesex, England

La Symphonie pastorale first published 1919
Isabelle first published 1911
These translations first published as *Two Symphonies* by Cassell 1931
Published in Penguin Books 1963
Reprinted in Penguin Classics 2001

1

Translation copyright 1931 by Dorothy Bussy
All rights reserved

Printed in Great Britain by Antony Rowe Ltd, Chippenham, Wiltshire
Set in Linotype Granjon

CONTENTS

LA SYMPHONIE PASTORALE

To Jean Schlumberger

FIRST NOTEBOOK

writing in 1st person — I we're in his thoughts, very personal + familiar experiencing it everything firsthand.

writes like a diary

10 February 189—

THE snow has been falling continuously for the last three days and all the roads are blocked. It has been impossible for me to go to R ..., where I have been in the habit of holding a service twice a month for the last fifteen years. This morning not more than thirty of my flock were gathered together in La Brévine chapel. *religious talk*

I will take advantage of the leisure this enforced confinement affords me to think over the past and to set down how I came to take charge of Gertrude.

I proposed to write here the whole history of her formation and development, for I seem to have called up out of the night her sweet and pious soul for no other end but adoration and love. Blessed be the Lord for having entrusted me with this task! *very unctious.*

Two years and six months ago, I had just driven back one afternoon from La Chaux-de-Fonds, when a little girl, who was a stranger to me, came up in a great hurry to fetch me to a place about five miles off, where she said an old woman lay dying. My horse was still in the shafts, so I made the child get into the carriage, and set off at once, after having first provided myself with a lantern, as I thought it very likely I should not be able to get back before dark.

I had supposed myself to be perfectly acquainted with the whole countryside in the neighbourhood of my parish; but when we had passed La Saudraie farm, the child made me take a road which I had never ventured down before. About two miles farther on, however, I recognized on the left-hand side a mysterious little lake, where I had sometimes

sign – d new things to come.
Fresh desire resurface.

LA SYMPHONIE PASTORALE

been to skate as a young man. I had not seen it for fifteen years, for none of my pastoral duties take me that way; I could not have said where it lay and it had so entirely dropped out of my mind that when I suddenly recognized it in the golden enchantment of the rose-flecked evening sky, I felt as though I had only seen it before in a dream.

he's going to enter a dream he is not in reality

The road ran alongside the stream that falls out of the lake, cut across the extreme end of the forest and then skirted a peat-moss. I had certainly never been there before.

The sun was setting and for a long time we had been driving in silence, when my young guide pointed out a cottage on the hill-side, which would have seemed uninhabited but for a tiny thread of smoke that rose from the chimney, looking blue in the shade and brightening as it reached the gold of the sky. I tied the horse up to an apple tree close by and then followed the child into the dark room where the old woman had just died.

The gravity of the landscape, the silence and solemnity of the hour struck me to the heart. A woman, apparently still in her youth, was kneeling beside the bed. The child, whom I had taken to be the deceased woman's granddaughter, but who was only her servant, lighted a smoky tallow tip and then stood motionless at the foot of the bed. During our long drive I had tried to get her to talk, but had not succeeded in extracting two words from her.

The kneeling woman rose. She was not a relation, as I had at first supposed, but only a neighbour, a friend whom the servant girl had fetched when she saw her mistress's strength failing, and who now offered to watch by the dead body. The old woman, she said, had passed away painlessly. We agreed together on the arrangements for the burial and the funeral service. As often before in this out-of-the-world country, it fell to me to settle everything. I was a little un-

they're not part of reality – another sign.

easy, I admit, at leaving the house, in spite of the poverty of its appearance, in the sole charge of this neighbour and of the little servant girl. But it seemed very unlikely that there was any treasure hidden away in the corner of this wretched dwelling ... and what else could I do? I inquired nevertheless whether the old woman had left any heirs.

Upon this, the woman took the tallow dip and held it up so as to light the corner of the hearth, and I could make out, crouching in the fireplace, and apparently asleep, a nondescript-looking creature, whose face was entirely hidden by a thick mass of hair.

'The blind girl there. She's a niece, the servant says. That's all that's left of the family, it seems. She must be sent to the workhouse; I don't see what else can be done with her.'

I was shocked to hear the poor thing's future disposed of in this way in her presence, and afraid such rough words might give her pain.

'Don't wake her up,' I said softly, as a hint to the woman that she should at any rate lower her voice.

'Oh, I don't think she's asleep. But she's an idiot. She can't speak or understand anything, I'm told. I have been in the room since the morning and she has hardly so much as stirred. I thought at first she was deaf; the servant thinks not, but the old woman was deaf herself and never uttered a word to her, nor to anyone else; she hadn't opened her mouth for a long time past except to eat and drink.'

'How old is she?'

'About fifteen, I suppose. But as to that, I know no more about it than you do. ...'

It did not immediately occur to me to take charge of the poor, forlorn creature myself; but after I had prayed – or, to be more accurate, while I was still praying on my knees between the woman and the little servant girl, who were both kneeling too – it suddenly came upon me that God had set a kind of obligation in my path, and that I could not shirk it without cowardice. When I rose, I had decided to take the girl away that very evening, though I had not actually asked myself what I should do with her afterwards, nor into whose charge I should put her. I stayed a few moments longer gazing at the old woman's sleeping face, with its puckered mouth, looking like a miser's purse with strings tightly drawn so as to let nothing escape. Then, turning towards the blind girl, I told the neighbour of my intention.

'Yes, it is better she should not be there tomorrow when they come to take the body away,' said she. And that was all.

Many things would be easily accomplished but for the imaginary objections men sometimes take a pleasure in inventing. From our childhood upwards, how often have we been prevented from doing one thing or another we should have liked to do, simply by hearing people about us repeat: 'He won't be able to! ...'

The blind girl allowed herself to be taken away like a lifeless block. The features of her face were regular, rather fine, but utterly expressionless. I took a blanket off the mattress where she must have usually slept, in a corner under a staircase that led from the room to the loft.

The neighbour was obliging and helped me to wrap her up carefully, for the night was very clear and chilly; after having lighted the carriage lamp, I started home, taking the girl with me. She sat huddled up against me – a soulless lump of flesh, with no sign of life beyond the communication of an obscure warmth. The whole way home I was thinking, 'Is she asleep? And what can this black sheep be like? ... And in what way do her waking hours differ from

12

pastor has a completely blank canvass to mould art to teach.

her sleeping? But this darkened body is surely tenanted; an immured soul is waiting there for a ray of Thy grace, O Lord, to touch it. Wilt Thou perhaps allow my love to dispel this dreadful darkness? ...

[handwritten: wants God to help him help her]

I have too much regard for the truth to pass over in silence the unpleasant welcome I had to encounter on my return home. My wife is a garden of all the virtues; and in the times of trouble we have sometimes gone through I have never for an instant had cause to doubt the stuff of which her heart is made; but it does not do to take her natural charity by surprise. She is an orderly person, careful neither to go beyond nor to fall short of her duty. Even her charity is measured, as though love were not an inexhaustible treasure. This is the only point on which we differ ...

[handwritten: is there more? he's not saying]

Her first thoughts, when she saw me bring home the poor girl that evening, broke from her in the following exclamation:

'What kind of job have you saddled yourself with now?'

As always happens when we have to come to an understanding, I began by telling the children – who were standing round, open-mouthed and full of curiosity and surprise – to leave the room. Ah! how different this welcome was from what I could have wished! Only my dear little Charlotte began to dance and clap her hands when she understood that something new, something alive was coming out of the carriage. But the others, who have been well trained by their mother, very soon damped the child's pleasure and made her fall into step.

[handwritten: the only one like him]

[handwritten: others are mother's children]

There was a moment of great confusion. And as neither my wife nor the children yet knew that they had to do with a blind person, they could not understand the extreme care with which I guided her footsteps. I myself was disconcerted by the odd moans the poor afflicted creature began

also needs.
to be trained.

to utter as soon as I let go her hand, which I had held in mine during the whole drive. There was nothing human in the sounds she made; they were more like the plaintive whines of a puppy. Torn away for the first time as she had been from the narrow round of customary sensations that had formed her universe, her knees now failed her; but when I pushed forward a chair, she sank on to the floor in a heap, as if she were incapable of sitting down; I now led her up to the fireplace and she regained her calm a little as soon as she was able to crouch down in the same position in which I had first seen her beside the old woman's fire, leaning against the chimney-piece. In the carriage, too, she had slipped off the seat and spent the whole drive huddled up at my feet. My wife, however, whose instinctive impulses are always the best, came to my help; it is her reflection which is constantly at odds with her heart and very often gets the better of it.

we are as
charitable

'What do you mean to do with *that*?' she asked when the girl had settled down.

I shivered in my soul at this use of the word 'that', and had some difficulty in restraining a movement of indignation. As, however, I was still under the spell of my long and peaceful meditation, I controlled myself. Turning towards the whole party, who were standing round in a circle, I placed my hand on the blind girl's head and said as solemnly as I could:

biblical ref.

'I have brought back the lost sheep.' *also animal ref.*

But Amélie will not admit that there can be anything unreasonable or super-reasonable in the teaching of the Gospel. I saw she was going to object, and it was then I made a sign to Jacques and Sarah, who, as they are accustomed to our little conjugal differences and have not much natural curiosity (not enough, I often think), led the two younger children out of the room. Then, as my wife still remained silent and a little irritated, I thought, by the intruder's presence:

'You needn't mind speaking before her,' I said. 'The poor child doesn't understand.'

Upon this Amélie began to protest that she had absolutely nothing to say – which is her usual prelude to the lengthiest explanations – and there was nothing for her to do but to submit, as usual, to all my most unpractical vagaries, however contrary to custom and good sense they might be. I have already said that I had not in the least made up my mind what I was going to do with the child. It had not occurred to me, or only in the vaguest way, that there was any possibility of taking her into our house permanently, and I may almost say it was Amélie herself who first suggested it to me, by asking whether I didn't think 'there were enough of us in the house already'? Then she declared that I always hurried on ahead without taking any thought for those who could not keep up with me, that for her part she considered five children quite enough and that since the birth of Claude (who at that very moment set up a howl from his cradle, as if he had heard his name) she had as much as she could put up with and that she couldn't stand any more.

At the beginning of her outburst, some of Christ's words rose from my heart to my lips; I kept them back, however, for I never think it becoming to allege the authority of the Holy Book as an excuse for my conduct. But when she spoke of her fatigue, I was struck with confusion, for I must admit it has more than once happened to me to let my wife suffer from the consequences of my impulsive and inconsiderate zeal. In the meantime, however, her recriminations had enlightened me as to my duty; I begged Amélie, therefore, as mildly as possible, to consider whether she would not have done the same in my place and whether she could have possibly abandoned a creature who had been so obviously left without anyone to help her; I added that I was under no illusions as to the extra fatigue the charge of this new inmate would add to the cares of the household, and that I regretted I was not more often able to help her with them. In this way I pacified her as best I could, begging her at the same time not to visit her anger on the innocent girl, who had done nothing to deserve it. Then I pointed out that Sarah was now old enough to be more of a help to her and that Jacques was no longer in need of her care. In short, God put into my mouth the right words to help her to accept what I am sure she would have undertaken of her own accord, if the circumstances had given her time to reflect and if I had not forestalled her decision without consulting her.

I thought the cause was almost gained, and my dear Amélie was already approaching Gertrude with the kindest intentions; but her irritation suddenly blazed up again higher than ever when, on taking up the lamp to look at the child more closely, she discovered her to be in a state of unspeakable dirt.

'Why, she's filthy!' she cried. 'Go and brush yourself quickly. No, not here. Go and shake your clothes outside. Oh dear! Oh dear! The children will be covered with them. There's nothing in the world I hate so much as vermin.'

It cannot be denied that the poor child was crawling with them; and I could not prevent a feeling of disgust as I thought how close I had kept her to me during our long drive.

When I came back a few minutes later, having cleaned myself as best I could, I found my wife had sunk into an arm-chair and with her head in her hands was giving way to a fit of sobbing.

'I did not mean to put your fortitude to such a test,' I said tenderly. 'In any case it is late tonight and too dark to do anything. I will sit up and keep the fire in and the child can sleep beside it. Tomorrow we will cut her hair and clean her properly. You need not attend to her until you have got over your repugnance.' And I begged her not to say anything to the children.

It was supper-time. My protégée, at whom our old Rosalie cast many a scowling glance as she waited on us, greedily devoured the plateful of soup I handed her. The meal was silent. I should have liked to talk to the children and to have touched their hearts by making them understand and feel the strangeness of such a condition of total deprivation. I should have liked to rouse their pity, their sympathy for the guest God had sent us; but I was afraid of reviving Amélie's irritation. It seemed as though the word had been passed to take no notice of what had happened and to forget all about it, though certainly not one of us can have been thinking of anything else.

I was extremely touched when, more than an hour after everyone had gone to bed and Amélie had left me, I saw my little Charlotte steal gently through the half-open door in her nightdress and bare feet; she flung her arms round my neck and hugged me fiercely.

'I didn't say good night to you properly,' she murmured.

Then, pointing with her little forefinger to the blind girl, who was now peacefully slumbering and whom she had been curious to see again before going to sleep:

'Why didn't I kiss her too?' she whispered.

'You shall kiss her tomorrow. We must let her be now. She is asleep,' I said, as I went with her to the door.

Then I sat down again and worked till morning, reading or preparing my next sermon.

'Certainly,' I remember thinking to myself, 'Charlotte

seems much more affectionate than the elder children, but when they were her age, I believe they all got round me too. My big boy Jacques, nowadays so distant and reserved ... One thinks them tender-hearted, when really they are only coaxing and wheedling one.'

27 February

The snow fell heavily again last night. The children are delighted, because they say we shall soon be obliged to go out by the windows. It is a fact that this morning the front door is blocked and the only way out is by the wash-house. Yesterday I made sure the village was sufficiently provisioned, for we shall doubtless remain cut off from the rest of the world for some time to come. This is not the first winter we have been snowbound, but I cannot remember ever having seen so thick a fall. I take advantage of it to go on with the tale I began yesterday.

I have said that when I first brought home this afflicted child I had not clearly thought out what place she would take in our household. I knew the limits of my wife's powers of endurance; I knew the size of our house and the smallness of our income. I had acted, as usual, in the way that was natural to me, quite as much as on principle, and without for a moment calculating the expense into which my impulse might land me – a proceeding I have always thought contrary to the Gospels' teachings. But it is one thing to trust one's cares to God and quite another to shift them on to other people. I soon saw I had laid a heavy burden on Amélie's shoulders – so heavy that at first I felt struck with shame.

I helped her as best I could to cut the little girl's hair, and I saw that she did even that with disgust. But when it came to washing and cleaning her, I was obliged to leave it to my wife; and I realized that I perforce escaped the heaviest and most disagreeable tasks.

18

[handwritten top margin: she helped Gertrude + then Pastor takes her 4 a ride.]

For the rest, Amélie ceased to make the slightest objection. She seemed to have thought things over during the night and resigned herself to her new duties; she even seemed to take some pleasure in them and I saw her smile when she had finished washing and dressing Gertrude. After her head had been shaved and I had rubbed it with ointment, a white cap was put on her; some of Sarah's old clothes and some clean linen took the place of the wretched rags Amélie threw into the fire. The name of Gertrude was chosen by Charlotte and immediately adopted by us all, in our ignorance of her real name, which the orphan girl herself was unaware of, and which I did not know how to find out. She must have been a little younger than Sarah, whose last year's clothes fitted her.

I must here confess the profound and overwhelming disappointment I felt during the first days. I had certainly built up a whole romance for myself on the subject of Gertrude's education, and the reality was a cruel disillusion. The indifference, the apathy of her countenance, or rather its total lack of expression froze my good intentions at their very source. She sat all day long by the fireside, seemingly on the defensive, and as soon as she heard our voices, still more when we came near her, her features appeared to harden; from being expressionless they became hostile; if anyone tried to attract her attention, she began to groan and grunt like an animal. This sulkiness only left her at mealtimes. I helped her myself and she flung herself on her food with a kind of bestial avidity which was most distressing to witness. And as love responds to love, so a feeling of aversion crept over me at this obstinate withholding of her soul. Yes, truly, I confess that at the end of the first ten days I had begun to despair, and my interest in her was even so far diminished that I almost regretted my first impulse and wished I had never brought her home with me.

[handwritten right margin: like Proust – have an image in mind + reality doesn't match.]

[handwritten left margin: always acted like an animal]

[handwritten bottom margin: like Odette – can't offer him what he "conjured" in his mind. — he regrets his decision.]

19

And the absurd thing was that Amélie, being not unnaturally a little triumphant over feelings I was really unable to hide from her, seemed all the more lavish of care and kindness now that she saw Gertrude was becoming a burden to me, and that I felt her presence among us as a mortification.

This was how matters stood when I received a visit from my friend, Dr Martins of Val Travers, in the course of one of his rounds. He was very much interested by what I told him of Gertrude's condition and was at first greatly astonished she should be so backward, considering her only infirmity was blindness; but I explained that in addition to this she had to suffer from the deafness of the old woman who was her sole guardian and who never spoke to her, so that the poor child had been utterly neglected. He persuaded me that in that case I was wrong to despair, but that I was not employing the proper method.

'You are trying to build,' he said, 'before making sure of your foundations. You must reflect that her whole mind is in a state of chaos and that even its first lineaments are as yet unformed. The first thing to be done is to make her connect together one or two sensations of touch and taste and attach a sound to them – a word – to serve as a kind of label. This you must repeat over and over again indefatigably and then try and get her to say it after you.

'Above all, don't go too quickly; take her at regular hours and never for very long at a time. . . .

'For the rest, this method,' he added, after having described it to me minutely, 'has nothing particularly magic about it. I did not invent it and other people have applied it. Don't you remember in the philosophy class at school, our professors told us of an analogous case *à propos* of Condillac and his animated statue . . . unless,' he corrected himself, 'I read it later in a psychological review . . . never

20

mind; I was struck by it and I even remember the name of the poor girl, who was still more afflicted than Gertrude, for she was a deaf-mute as well as blind. She was discovered somewhere in England towards the middle of the last century by a doctor who devoted himself to educating her. Her name was Laura Bridgeman. The doctor kept a journal, as you ought to do, of the child's progress – or rather, in the first place, of his efforts to instruct her. For days and weeks he went on, first making her feel alternately two little objects, a pin and a pen, and then putting her fingers on the two words "pin" and "pen" written in a Braille book for the blind. For weeks and weeks there was no result. Her body seemed quite vacant. He did not lose courage, however. "I felt like a person," says he, "leaning over the edge of a deep dark well and desperately dangling a rope in the hopes a hand would catch hold of it." For he did not for one moment doubt that someone was there at the bottom of the well and that in the end the rope would be caught hold of. And one day, at last, he saw Laura's impassive face light up with a kind of smile. I can well believe that tears of love and gratitude sprang to his eyes and that he straightway fell on his knees and gave thanks to God. Laura had understood at last what it was the doctor wanted. She was saved! From that day forward she was all attention; her progress was rapid; she was soon able to learn by herself and eventually became the head of an institution for the blind – unless that was some other person – for there have been other cases recently which the reviews and newspapers have been full of; they were all astonished – rather foolishly, in my opinion – that such creatures should be happy. For it is a fact that all these walled-up prisoners were happy, and as soon as they were able to express anything, it was their *happiness* they spoke of. The journalists of course went into ecstasies and pointed the "moral" for people who "enjoy" all their five senses and yet have the audacity to complain ...'

Here an argument arose between Martins and me, for I objected to his pessimism and could not allow what he seemed to infer – that our senses serve in the long run only to make us miserable.

'That's not what I meant,' he protested; 'I merely wanted to say – first, that man's spirit imagines beauty, comfort and harmony more easily and gladly than it can the disorder and sin which everywhere tarnish, stain, degrade and mar this world – and further, that this state of things is revealed to us by our senses, which also help us to contribute to it. So that I feel inclined to put the words *"si sua mala nescient"* after Virgil's *"Fortunatos nimium"*, instead of *"si sua bona norint"* as we are taught. How happy men would be if they knew nothing of evil!'

Then he told me of one of Dickens's stories – which he thinks was directly inspired by Laura Bridgeman's case; he promised to send it to me, and four days later I received *The Cricket on the Hearth*, which I read with the greatest pleasure. It is a rather lengthy but at times very touching tale of a little blind girl, maintained by her father, a poor toy-maker, in an illusory world of comfort, wealth and happiness. Dickens exerts all his art in representing this deception as an act of piety, but, thank Heaven, I shall not have to make use of any such falsehood with Gertrude.

The day after Martins's visit, I began to put his method into practice with all the application I was capable of. I am sorry now I did not take notes, as he advised, of Gertrude's first steps along the twilit path where I myself at first was but a groping guide. During the first weeks more patience was needed than can well be believed, not only because of the amount of time an education of this kind requires, but also

because of the reproaches it brought me. It is painful for
me to have to say that these reproaches came from Amélie;
but for that matter, if I mention this here, it is because it has
not left in me the slightest trace of animosity or bitterness
– I declare this most solemnly, in case these lines should
come to her eyes later on. (Does not Christ's teaching of the
forgiveness of injuries follow immediately after the parable
of the lost sheep?) More than that – at the very moment
when I most suffered from her reproaches, I could not feel
angry with her for disapproving the length of time I devoted to Gertrude. What I chiefly deplored was that she
failed to believe that my efforts would be at all successful.
Yes, it was her want of faith that grieved me – without,
however, discouraging me. How often I heard her repeat:
'If only any good were to come of it all ...' And she remained stubbornly convinced that my work was labour lost;
so that naturally she thought it wrong of me to devote the
time to Gertrude's education which she always declared
would have been better employed otherwise. And whenever I was occupied with Gertrude, she managed to make
out that I was wanted at that moment for someone or
something else, and that I was giving her time that ought
to have been given to others. In fact, I think she felt a kind
of maternal jealousy, for she more than once said to me:
'You never took so much pains with any of your own
children,' – which was true; for though I am very fond of
my children, I have never thought it my business to take
much pains with them.

It has often been my experience that the parable of the
lost sheep is one of the most difficult of acceptance for
certain people, who yet believe themselves to be profoundly
Christian at heart. That each single sheep of the flock
should be in turn more precious in the eyes of the shepherd
than the rest of the flock as a whole, is beyond and above

23

[handwritten margin note at top: move attention put on her because she's needs help than his own children who don't]

[handwritten left margin: Gertrude has just gone astray + needs to be brought back]

their power of conception. And the words, 'If a man have a hundred sheep and one of them be gone astray, doth he not leave the ninety and nine and goeth into the mountains and seeketh that which is gone astray' – words all aglow with charity, such persons would, if they dared speak frankly, declare to be abominably unjust.

Gertrude's first smiles consoled me for everything and repaid me for my pains a hundred-fold. For 'and if so be that he find it, verily I say unto you, he rejoiceth more of that sheep, than of the ninety and nine which went not astray'. Yes, verily, the smile that dawned for me one morning on that marble face of hers, when she seemed suddenly touched to understanding and interest by what I had been trying for so many days to teach her, flooded my heart with a more seraphic joy than was ever given me by any child of my own.

[handwritten: more rewarding because she was such a challenge]

5 March

I noted this date as if it had been a birthday. It was not so much a smile as a transfiguration. Her features flashed into life – a sudden illumination, like the crimson glow that precedes dawn in the high Alps, thrilling the snowy peak on which it lights and calling it up out of darkness – such a flood, it seemed, of mystic colour; and I thought too of the pool of Bethesda at the moment the angel descends to stir the slumbering water. A kind of ecstasy rapt me at sight of the angelic expression that came over Gertrude's face so suddenly, for it was clear to me that this heavenly visitor was not so much intelligence as love. And in a very transport of gratitude I kissed her forehead and felt that I was offering thanks to God.

[handwritten left margin: still very charitable + religious.]

The progress she made after this was as rapid as the first steps had been slow. It is only with an effort that I can now recall our manner of proceeding; it seemed to me some-

24

times that Gertrude advanced by leaps and bounds, as though in defiance of all method. I can remember that at first I dwelt more on the qualities of objects than on their variety – hot, cold, sweet, bitter, rough, soft, light; and then on actions – to pick up, to put down, to remove, to approach, to tie, to cross, to assemble, to disperse, etc. ... And very soon I abandoned all attempt at method and began to talk to her without troubling much as to whether her mind was always able to follow me; but I went slowly, inviting and provoking her questions as she seemed inclined. Certainly her mind was at work during the hours I left her to herself; for every time I came back to her after an absence, it was to find with fresh surprise that the wall of darkness that separated us had grown less thick. After all, I said to myself, it is so that the warmth of the air and the insistence of spring gradually triumph over winter. How often have I wondered at the melting of the snow; its white cloak seems to wear thin from underneath, while to all appearance it remains unchanged. Every winter Amélie falls into the trap: 'The snow is as thick as ever,' she declares. And indeed it still seems so, when all at once there comes a break and suddenly, in patches here and there, life once more shows through.

Fearing that Gertrude might become peaky if she continued to sit beside the fire like an old woman, I began to make her go out. But she refused to do this unless she held my arm. I realized from her surprise and fear when she first left the house, and before she was able to tell me so in words, that she had never as yet ventured out of doors. In the cottage where I had found her no one had cared for her further than to give her food and prevent her from dying – for I cannot say that anyone helped her to live. Her little universe of darkness was bounded by the walls of the single room she never left; she scarcely ventured on summer days

25

as far as the threshold, when the door stood open to the great universe of light. She told me later that when she heard the birds' song she used to suppose it was simply the effect of light, like the gentle warmth which she felt on her cheeks and hands, and that, without precisely thinking about it, it seemed to her quite natural that the warm air should begin to sing, just as the water begins to boil on the fire. The truth is she did not trouble to think; she took no interest in anything and lived in a state of frozen numbness till the day I took charge of her. I remember her inexhaustible delight when I told her that the little voices came from living creatures, whose sole function, apparently, was to express the joy that lies broadcast throughout all nature. (It was from that day that she began to say, 'I am as joyful as a bird.') And yet the idea that these songs proclaim the splendours of a spectacle she could not behold had begun by making her melancholy.

'Is the world really as beautiful as the birds say?' she would ask. 'Why do people not tell us so oftener? Why do *you* never tell me so? Is it for fear of grieving me because I cannot see it? That would be wrong. I listen so attentively to the birds; I think I understand everything they say.'

'People who can see do not hear them as well as you do, my Gertrude,' I said, hoping to comfort her.

'Why don't other animals sing?' she went on. Sometimes her questions surprised me and left me perplexed for a moment, for she forced me to reflect on things I had hitherto taken for granted. It was thus it occurred to me for the first time that the closer an animal lives to the ground and the heavier its weight, the duller it is. I tried to make her understand this; and I told her of the squirrel and its gambols.

She asked me if the birds were the only animals that flew.

'There are butterflies too.'

'And do they sing?'

26

'They have another way of telling their joy. It is painted on their wings . . .'
And I described the rainbow colours of the butterfly.

28 February

Now let me turn back a little, for yesterday I allowed myself to be carried away.

In order to teach Gertrude, I had had to learn the Braille alphabet myself; but she was soon able to read much quicker than I could; I had some difficulty in deciphering the writing, and besides found it easier to follow with my eyes than with my fingers. For that matter, I was not the only one to give her lessons. And at first I was glad to be helped in this respect, for I have a great deal to do in the parish, the houses being so widely scattered that my visits to the poor and the sick sometimes oblige me to go far afield. Jacques had managed to break his arm while skating during the Christmas holidays, which he was spending with us; for during term time he goes to Lausanne, where he received his early education, and where he is studying at the Faculty of Theology. The fracture was not serious and Martins, whom I at once sent for, was easily able to set it without the help of a surgeon; but it was considered advisable for Jacques to keep indoors for some time. He now suddenly began to take an interest in Gertrude, to whom he had hitherto paid no attention, and occupied himself with helping me to teach her to read. His assistance only lasted the time of his convalescence – about three weeks – but during those weeks Gertrude's progress was very marked. She was now fired with extraordinary zeal. Her young intelligence, but yesterday so benumbed and torpid, its first steps hardly taken and scarcely able to walk, seemed now already preparing to run. I wondered at the ease with which she succeeded in formulating her thoughts and at the rapidity with which she learnt

27

to express herself – not childishly, but at once correctly, conveying her ideas by the help of images, taken in the most delightful and unexpected way from the objects we had just taught her to recognize, or from others we described to her, when we could not actually put them within her grasp; for she always used things she could touch or feel in order to explain what was beyond her reach, after the method of land-surveyors measuring distances.

But I think it is unnecessary to note here all the first steps of her education, doubtless the same in the early education of all blind people. I suppose too that in each case the teacher must have been plunged into a similar perplexity by the questions of colours. (And this subject led me to the reflection that there is nowhere any mention of colours in the Gospels.) I do not know how other people set about it; for my part, I began by naming the colours of the prism to her in the order in which they occur in the rainbow; but then a confusion was immediately set up in her mind between colour and brightness; and I realized that her imagination was unable to draw any distinction between the *quality* of the shade and what painters, I believe, call its '*value*'. She had the greatest difficulty in understanding that every colour in its turn might be more or less dark and that they might be mixed one with the other to an unlimited extent. It puzzled her exceedingly, and she came back to the subject again and again.

About this time the opportunity was given me of taking her to a concert at Neuchâtel. The part played by each instrument in the symphony suggested to me the idea of recurring to this question of colours. I bade Gertrude observe the different resonances of the brasses, the strings and the wood instruments, and that each of them was able in its own way to produce the whole series of sounds, from the lowest to the highest, with varying intensity. I asked her to

28

imagine the colours of nature in the same way – the reds and oranges analogous to the sounds of the horns and trombones; the yellows and greens like those of the violins, cellos, and double basses; the violets and blues suggested by the clarinets and oboes. A sort of inner rapture now took the place of all her doubts and uncertainties.

'How beautiful it must be!' she kept on repeating.

Then suddenly she added, 'But the white? I can't understand now what the white can be like.'

And I at once saw how insecure my comparison was.

'White,' I tried however to explain, 'is the extreme treble limit where all the tones are blended into one, just as black is the bass or dark limit.'

But this did not satisfy me any more than it did her; and she pointed out at once that the wood instruments, the brasses and the violins remain distinct in the bass as well as in the treble parts. How often I have been obliged to remain puzzled and silent, as I did then, searching about for some comparison I might appeal to.

'Well,' said I at last, 'imagine white as something absolutely pure, something in which colour no longer exists, but only light; and black, on the contrary, something so full of colour that it has become dark . . .'

I recall this fragment of dialogue merely as an example of the difficulties which I encountered only too often. Gertrude had this good point, that she never pretended to understand, as so many people do, thus filling their minds with inaccurate or false statements, which in the end vitiate all their reasoning. So long as she could not form a clear idea of any notion, it remained a cause of anxiety and discomfort to her.

As regards what I have just related, the/difficulty was increased by the fact that the notion of light and that of heat began by being closely associated with each other in

She challenges him by Questioning what he thinks he knows

light + heat

1

·her mind, and I had the greatest trouble afterwards in dis-
connecting them.

Thus, through these experiments with her, it was constantly brought home to me how greatly the visual world
differs from the world of sound, and that any comparison
between the two must necessarily be a lame one.

29 February

I have been so full of my comparisons that I have not yet
said what immense pleasure the Neuchâtel concert gave
Gertrude. It was actually the *Pastoral Symphony* that was
being played! I say *actually* because, as will be easily understood, there is no work I could have more wished her to
hear. For a long time after we had left the concert-room,
Gertrude remained silent, as though lost in ecstasy.

'Is what you see really as beautiful as that?' she asked at
last.

'As beautiful as what, dear child?'

she can picture the music

'As that "scene on the bank of a stream"?'

her clever-ness — she appreciates things more than life.

I did not answer at once, for I was reflecting that those
ineffable harmonies painted the world as it might have
been, as it would be without evil and without sin, rather
than the world as it really was. And I had never yet ventured
to speak to Gertrude of evil and sin and death.

'Those who have eyes,' I said at last, 'do not know their
happiness.'

'But I who have not,' she cried, '*I* know the happiness
of hearing.'

She pressed up against me as she walked and hung on to
my arm in the way small children do.

'Pastor, do you feel how happy I am? No, no, I don't
say so to please you. Look at me. Can't you see on people's
faces whether they are speaking the truth? I always know
by their voices. Do you remember the day you answered

me that you weren't crying, when my aunt' (that is what she called my wife) 'had reproached you with being no help to her? And I cried out, "Pastor, that's not true!" Oh, I felt at once from your voice that you weren't telling me the truth; there was no need for me to feel your cheeks to know that you had been crying.' And she repeated very loud: 'No, there was no need for me to feel your cheeks' – which made me turn red, for we were still in the town and the passers-by turned round to look at us. She went on, however:

'You mustn't try to deceive me, you know. First of all because it would be very mean to try to deceive a blind person ... and then, because you wouldn't succeed,' she added laughing. 'Tell me, pastor, you aren't unhappy, are you?' I put her hand to my lips, as though to make her feel, without having to confess it, that part of my happiness came from her, and answered as I did so.

'No, Gertrude, I am not unhappy. How should I be unhappy?'

'And yet you cry sometimes?'

'I have cried sometimes.'

'Not since that time?'

'No, I have not cried since that time.'

'And you have not felt inclined to cry?'

'No, Gertrude.'

'And ... tell me, have you felt inclined since then not to speak the truth?'

'No, dear child.'

'Can you promise never to try to deceive me?'

'I promise.'

'Well, tell me quickly then – am I pretty?'

This sudden question dumbfounded me ... all the more because I had studiously avoided up till then taking any notice of Gertrude's undeniable beauty; and moreover I considered it perfectly unnecessary that she should be informed of it herself.

'What can it matter to you?' I said.

'I am anxious ...' she went on, 'I am anxious to know whether I do not ... how shall I put it? ... make too much of a discord in the symphony. Whom else should I ask, pastor?'

'It is not a pastor's business to concern himself with the beauty of people's faces,' said I, defending myself as best I could.

'Why not?'

'Because the beauty of their souls suffices him.'

'You had rather I thought myself ugly,' was her reply, with a charming pout; so that, giving up the struggle, I exclaimed:

'Gertrude, you know quite well you are pretty.'

She was silent and her face took on an expression of great gravity which did not leave her until we got home.

stark contrast

On our return Amélie at once managed to make me feel she disapproved of the way I had been spending my day. She might have told me so before; but she had let Gertrude and me start without a word, according to her habit of letting people do things and of reserving to herself the right to blame them afterwards. For that matter, she did not actually reproach me; but her very silence was accusing; for surely it would have been natural to have inquired what we had heard, since she knew I was taking Gertrude to the concert. Would not the child's pleasure have been increased if she had felt that the smallest interest had been taken in it? But Amélie did not remain entirely silent – she merely seemed to put a sort of affectation into avoiding any but the most indifferent topics; and it was not till evening, when the little ones had gone to bed, and after I had asked her in

He's happy with Gertrude – she makes him happy. But his wife doesn't seem to.

private and with some severity if she was vexed with me for taking Gertrude to the concert, that I got the following answer:

'You do things for her you would never have done for any of your own children.') true

So it was always the same grievance, and the same refusal to understand that the feast is prepared for the child who returns to us – not for those who have stayed at home ... as we read in the parable. It grieved me too to see that she took no account of Gertrude's infirmity – poor Gertrude, who could hope for no other kind of pleasure. And if I providentially happened to be free that afternoon – I, who am as a rule so much in request – Amélie's reproach was all the more unfair, because she knew perfectly well that the other children were busy or occupied in one way or another, and that she herself did not care for music, so that even if *his wife* she had all the time in the world, it would never enter her head to go to a concert, not even if it were given at our very door.

What distressed me still more was that Amélie had actually said this in front of Gertrude; for though I had taken my wife on one side, she had raised her voice so much that Gertrude heard her. I felt not so much sad as indignant, and a few moments later, when Amélie had left us, I went up to Gertrude and taking her frail little hand in mine, I lifted it to my face. 'You see,' I said, 'this time I am not crying.' *fact that his wife's anger turns him to Gertrude more*

'No,' answered she, trying to smile, 'this time it is my turn.' And as she looked up at me, I suddenly saw her face was flooded with tears.

8 March

The only pleasure I can give Amélie is to refrain from doing the things she dislikes. These very negative signs of love are the only ones she allows me. The degree to which she has already narrowed my life is a thing she cannot realize.

33 *bad relations here – make him turn to Gertrude*

like Gertrude

Oh, would to Heaven she would demand something difficult of me! How gladly I would undertake a rash – a dangerous task for her! But she seems to have a repugnance for everything that is not usual; so that for her, progress in life consists merely in adding like days to like days. She does not desire – she will not even accept – any new virtue, nor even an increase of the old ones. When it is not with disapproval, it is with mistrust that she views every effort of the soul to find in Christianity something other than the domestication of our instincts.

I must confess that I entirely forgot, that afternoon at Neuchâtel, to go and pay our haberdasher's bill and to bring her back some reels of cotton she wanted. But I was more vexed with myself for this than she could have been; especially as I had been quite determined not to forget her commissions, being very well aware that 'he that is faithful in that which is least is faithful also in much', and being afraid too of the conclusions she might draw from my forgetfulness. I should even have been glad if she had reproached me with it, for I certainly deserved reproaches. But, as often happens, the imaginary grievance outweighed the definite charge. Ah! how beautiful life would be and how bearable our wretchedness if we were content with real evils, without opening the doors to the phantoms and monsters of our imagination. ... But I am straying here into observations that would do better as the subject of a sermon – (Luke xii. 29: 'Neither be ye of doubtful mind'). It is the history of Gertrude's intellectual and moral development that I purposed tracing here and I must now return to it.

I had hoped to follow its course step by step in this book and had begun to tell the story in detail. Not only, however, do I lack time to note all its phases with minuteness, but I find it extremely difficult at the present moment to remember their exact sequence. Carried away by my tale, I began by setting down remarks of Gertrude's and conversations with her that are far more recent; a person reading these pages would no doubt be astonished at hearing her express herself so justly and reason so judiciously in such a little while. The fact is her progress was amazingly rapid; I often wondered at the promptness with which her mind fastened on the intellectual food I offered it, and indeed on everything it could catch hold of, absorbing it all by a constant process of assimilation and maturation. The way in which she forestalled my thoughts and outstripped them was a continual surprise to me, and often from one lesson to another I ceased to recognize my pupil.

At the end of a very few months there was no appearance of her intelligence having lain dormant for so long. Even at this early stage she showed more sense and judgement than the generality of young girls, distracted as they are by the outside world and prevented from giving their best attention by a multitude of futile preoccupations. She was, moreover, a good deal older, I think, than we had at first supposed. Indeed it seemed as though she were determined to profit by her blindness, so that I actually wondered whether this infirmity was not in many ways an advantage. In spite of myself I compared her to Charlotte, so easily distracted by the veriest trifles, so that many a time while hearing the child her lessons, as I sometimes did, I found myself thinking, 'Dear me! How much better she would listen, if only she could not see!'

Needless to say, Gertrude was a very eager reader, but as I wished as far as possible to keep in touch with the development of her mind, I preferred her not to read too much – or at any rate not much without me – and especially not the Bible – which may seem very strange for a Protestant. I will explain myself; but before touching on a question so important, I wish to relate a small circumstance which is

35

connected with music and which should be placed, as far as I can remember, shortly after the concert at Neuchâtel.

Yes, the concert, I think, took place three weeks before the summer holidays which brought Jacques home. In the meantime I had often sat with Gertrude at the little harmonium of our chapel which is usually played by Mlle de la M ..., with whom Gertrude is at present staying. Louise de la M ... had not yet begun to give Gertrude music lessons. Notwithstanding my love of music, I do not know much about it, and I felt very little able to teach her anything when I sat beside her at the keyboard.

'No,' she had said after the first gropings, 'you had better leave me. I had rather try by myself.'

And I left her all the more willingly that the chapel did not seem to me a proper place in which to be shut up alone with her, as much out of respect for the sanctity of the place as for fear of gossip – though as a rule I endeavour to disregard it; in this case, however, it is a matter that concerns not only me but her. So when a round of visits called me in that direction, I would take her to the church and leave her there, often for long hours together, and then would fetch her away on my return. In this way she spent her time patiently hunting out harmonies, and I would find her again towards evening, pondering over some concord of sounds which had plunged her into a long ecstasy.

On one of the first days of August, barely more than six months ago, it so happened that I had gone to visit a poor widow in need of consolation, and had not found her in. I therefore returned at once to fetch Gertrude from the church where I had left her; she was not expecting me back so soon, and I was extremely surprised to find Jacques with her. Neither of them heard me come in, for the little noise I made was covered by the sound of the organ. It is not in my nature to play the spy, but everything that touches Gertrude

[handwritten marginal note: perhaps he feels guilty in church because he likes her]

very clear

touches me; so stepping as softly as I could, I stole up the few steps that lead to the gallery – an excellent post of observation. I must say that during the whole time I was there I did not hear a word from either of them that they might not have said before me. But he sat very close to her, *jealousy* and several times I saw him take her hand in order to guide her fingers over the keys. Was it not in itself strange that she should accept instructions and guidance from him, when she had previously refused them from me, preferring, she said, to practise by herself? I was more astonished, more pained than I liked to own, and was just on the point of intervening, when I saw Jacques suddenly take out his watch.

she likes Jacques

'I must leave you now,' he said, 'my father will be coming back in a moment.'

I saw him lift her unresisting hand to his lips; then he left. A few moments later I went noiselessly down the stairs and opened the church door so that she might hear me and think I had only just arrived.

'Well, Gertrude! Are you ready to come home? How is the organ getting on?'

'Very well,' she answered in the most natural tone; 'I have really made some progress today.' *because of Jacques*

A great sadness filled my heart, but we neither of us made any allusion to the episode I have just described.

I was impatient to find myself alone with Jacques. My wife, Gertrude and the children used as a rule to go to bed early after supper, while we two sat late over our studies. I was waiting for this moment. But before speaking to him, I felt my heart bursting with such a mixture of feelings that I could not – or dared not – begin on the subject that was tormenting me. And it was he who abruptly broke the silence by announcing his intention of spending the rest of the holidays with us. Now a few days earlier he had spoken to us about a tour he wanted to make in the high Alps – a

he likes her too

37

He's jealous that Gertrude let Jacques help her on piano + kissed her hand

plan my wife and I heartily approved of; I knew his friend
T . . ., who was to be his travelling companion, was counting on him; it was therefore quite obvious to me that this
sudden change of plan was not unconnected with the scene
I had just witnessed. I was at first stirred by violent indignation, but was afraid to give way to it lest it should put an
end to my son's confidence altogether; I was afraid too of
pronouncing words I should afterwards regret; so making
a great effort over myself, I said as naturally as I could:

'I thought T . . . was counting on you.'

'Oh,' he answered, 'not absolutely, and besides he will
have no difficulty in finding someone else to go with him.
I can rest here quite as well as in the Oberland, and I really
think I can spend my time better than mountaineering.'

'In fact,' I said, 'you have found something to occupy you
at home.'

He noticed some irony in the tone of my voice and looked
at me, but being unable as yet to guess the motive of it,
went on unconcernedly:

'You know I have always liked reading better than
climbing.'

'Yes, my dear boy,' said I, returning his glance with one
as searching; 'but are not lessons in harmonium playing
even more attractive than reading?'

No doubt he felt himself blush, for he put his hand to
his forehead, as though to shade his eyes from the lamplight, but he recovered himself almost immediately, and
went on in a voice I could have wished less steady:

'Do not blame me too much, Father. I did not mean to
hide anything from you and you have only forestalled by a
very little the confession I was preparing to make you.'

He spoke deliberately, as if he were reading the words
out of a book, finishing his sentences with as much calm
as if it were a matter in which he had no concern. The

38

He is behaving rashly + unusually — jealousy. Out of character.

FIRST NOTEBOOK

extraordinary self-possession he showed brought my ex-
asperation to a climax. Feeling that I was about to interrupt
him, he raised his hand, as much as to say, 'No, you can
speak afterwards; let me finish first.' But I seized his arm
and shook it.

'Oh,' I exclaimed impetuously, 'I would rather never
see you again than have you trouble the purity of Gertrude's
soul. I don't want your confessions! To abuse infirmity,
innocence, candour! What abominable cowardice! I should
never have thought you capable of it. And to speak of it *jealous*
with such cold-blooded unconcern! ... Understand me; it *of any*
is I who have charge of Gertrude and I will not suffer you *one*
to speak to her, to touch her, to see her for one single day *else*
more.' *possession — wants her 4 himself*

'But, Father,' he went on as calmly as ever, driving me *!*
almost beside myself, 'you may be sure that I respect Ger- *like*
trude as much as you do. You are making a strange mistake *in*
if you think there is anything reprehensible – I don't say in *Proust*
my conduct – but in my intentions and in my secret heart.
I love Gertrude and respect her, I tell you, as much as I love
her. The idea of troubling her, of abusing her innocence is
as abominable to me as to you.'

Then he protested that what he wanted was to be her
help, her friend, her husband; that he had thought he ought
not to speak to me about it until he had made up his mind
to marry her; that Gertrude herself did not know of his intention and that he had wanted to speak to me about it first.

'This is the confession I had to make to you,' he wound
up; 'and I have nothing else to confess, believe me.'

These words filled me with stupor. As I listened, I felt
my temples throbbing. I had been prepared with nothing
but reproaches, and the fewer grounds he gave me for indignation the more at a loss I felt, so that at the end of his
speech I had nothing left to say.

Jacques wants to marry her

no reason 4 him to be angry, except 4 jealousy

'Let us go to bed,' I said at last, after some moments of silence. 'Tomorrow I will tell you what I think about it all.'

'Tell me at any rate that you aren't still angry with me.'

'I must have the night to think it over.'

When I saw Jacques again the next morning, I seemed to be looking at him for the first time. I suddenly realized that my son was no longer a child but a young man: so long as I thought of him as a child, the love which I had accidentally discovered might appear monstrous. I had passed the whole night persuading myself that on the contrary it was perfectly natural and normal. Why was it that my dissatisfaction only became keener still? It was not till later that this became clear to me. In the meantime I had to speak to Jacques and tell him my decision. Now an instinct as sure as the voice of conscience warned me that this marriage must be prevented at all costs.

I took Jacques down to the bottom of the garden.

'Have you said anything to Gertrude?' I began by asking him.

'No,' he answered; 'perhaps she feels I love her, but I have not yet told her so.'

'Then you must promise me not to speak of it yet awhile.'

'I am determined to obey you, Father; but mayn't I know your reasons?'

I hesitated to give them, feeling doubtful whether those that first came into my mind were the wisest to put forward. To tell the truth, conscience rather than reason dictated my conduct.

'Gertrude is too young,' I said at last. 'You must reflect that she has not yet been confirmed. You know she was unhappily not like other children and did not begin to develop till very late. She is so trustful that she would no doubt be only too easily touched by the first words of love she heard.

(margin notes: he admits that he loves her + that it may be unnatural)

40

(bottom notes: So he takes advantage of her! He's scared she'll want Jacques.)

[handwritten marginalia top: "Pastor being totally selfish — not thinking of son or Gertrude"]

And that is why it is of importance not to say them. Your feelings, you say, are in no way reprehensible; I say they are wrong because they are premature. It is our duty to be prudent for Gertrude till she is able to be prudent for herself. It is a matter of conscience. *[handwritten: "— + his conscience?"]*

Jacques has one excellent point – that the simple words I often used to him as a child: 'I appeal to your conscience,' have always been sufficient to check him. Meanwhile, as I looked at him, I thought that if Gertrude were able to see, she could not fail to admire the tall slender figure, so straight and yet so lissom, the smooth forehead, the open look, the face, so childlike still, though now, as it were, overshadowed by a sudden gravity. He was bare-headed, and his fair hair, which was rather long at that time, curled a little at the temples and half hid his ears.

[handwritten left margin: "he's feeling threatened by son's youth too"]

'There is another thing I want to ask you,' I went on, rising from the bench where we had been sitting. 'You had intended, you said, to go away the day after tomorrow; I beg you not to put off your journey. You were to remain away a whole month at least; I beg you not to shorten your absence by a single day. Is that agreed?'

[handwritten right margin: "getting him out of the way"]

'Very well, Father, I will obey.'

[handwritten: "temptation – way to Gertrude"]

I thought he turned extremely pale – so pale that the colour left even his lips. But I persuaded myself that such prompt submission argued no very great love, and I felt inexpressibly relieved. I was touched besides by his obedience. 'That's the child I love,' I said gently. And drawing him to me, I put my lips to his forehead. There was a slight recoil on his part, but I refused to feel hurt by it.

[handwritten left margin: "justifying his actions again"]

10 March

Our house is so small that we are obliged to live more or less on top of one another, which is sometimes very inconvenient for my work, although I keep a little room for myself

like in El Sur – strong patriarcal figure – head of inside – rules one family

upstairs where I can receive my visitors in private – and especially inconvenient when I want to speak to one of the family in private, without such an air of solemnity as would be the case if the interview took place in this little parlour of mine, which the children call my 'sanctum' and into which they are forbidden to enter. On that particular morning, however, Jacques had gone to Neuchâtel to buy a pair of boots for his mountaineering, and as it was very fine, the children had gone out after lunch with Gertrude, whom they take charge of, while she at the same time takes charge of them. (It is a pleasure for me to note that Charlotte is particularly attentive to her.) At tea then, a meal we always take in the common sitting-room, I was quite naturally left alone with Amélie. This was just what I wanted, for I was longing to speak to her. It happens to me so rarely to have a *tête-à-tête* with her, that I felt almost shy, and the importance of what I had to say agitated me as much as if it had been a question not of Jacques's affairs but of my own. I felt too before I began to speak how two people who love one another and live practically the same life can yet remain (or become) as much of an enigma to each other as if they lived behind stone walls. Words in this case – those spoken or those heard – have the pathetic sound of vain knocking against the resistance of that dividing barrier, which, unless watch be kept, will grow more and more impenetrable. ...

here words are not enough compare to Proust's importance of words

'Jacques was speaking to me last night and again this morning,' I began, as she poured out the tea; and my voice was as faltering as Jacques' had been steady the day before. 'He told me he loved Gertrude.'

'It was quite right of him to tell you,' said she, without looking at me and continuing her housewifely task, as if I had said the most natural thing in the world – or rather as if I had said nothing she did not already know.

42

'He told me he wanted to marry her; he is resolved to . . .'

'It was only to be expected,' she murmured, with a slight shrug of her shoulders.

'Then you suspected it?' I asked in some vexation.

'I've seen it coming on for a long while. But that's the kind of thing men never notice.'

It would have been no use to protest, and besides there was perhaps some truth in her rejoinder, so, 'In that case,' I simply objected, 'you might have warned me.'

She gave me the little crooked smile with which she sometimes accompanies and screens her reticences, and then, with a sideways nod of her head:

'If I had to warn you,' she said, 'of everything you can't see for yourself, I should have my work cut out for me!'

What did she mean by this insinuation? I did not know or care to know, and went on, without attending to it:

'Well, but I want to hear what you think about it.'

She sighed. Then, 'You know, my dear, that I never approved of that child's staying with us.'

I found it difficult not to be irritated by her harking back in this way to the past.

'Her staying with us is not what we are discussing,' I said, but Amélie went on:

'I have always thought it would lead to no good.' *but perhaps didn't matter*

With a strong desire to be conciliatory, I caught at her phrase:

'Then you think it would be no good if it led to such a marriage? That's just what I wanted to hear you say. I am glad we are of the same opinion.' Then I added that Jacques had submitted quietly to the reasons I had given him, so that there was no need for her to be anxious; that it had been agreed he was to leave the next day for his trip and stay away a whole month.

'As I have no more wish than you that he should find

43

like father in el Ser — lost in his own world — can't see dangers. Loses contact with wife + children because of other woman.

Gertrude here when he comes back,' I wound up, 'I think the best thing would be to hand her over to the care of Mlle de la M ... and I could continue to see her there. For there's no denying that I have very serious obligations to her. I have just been to sound our friend and she is quite ready to oblige us. In this way you will be rid of a presence that is painful to you. Louise de la M ... will look after Gertrude; she seemed delighted with the arrangement; she is looking forward already to giving her harmony lessons.'

Amélie seemed determined to remain silent, so that I went on:

'As we shall not want Jacques to see Gertrude there, I think it would be a good thing to warn Mlle de la M ... of the state of affairs, don't you?'

I hoped by putting this question to get something out of her; but she kept her lips tightly shut, as if she had sworn not to speak. And I went on – not that I had anything more to add, but because I could not endure her silence:

'For that matter, perhaps Jacques will have got over his love by the time he gets back. At his age one hardly knows what one wants.'

'And even later one doesn't always know,' said she at last, rather oddly.

Her enigmatical and slightly oracular way of speaking irritated me, for I am too frank by nature to put up easily with mystery-making. Turning towards her, I begged her to explain what she meant to imply by that.

'Nothing, my dear,' she answered sadly. 'I was only thinking that a moment ago you were wishing to be warned of the things you didn't notice yourself.'

'Well?'

'Well, I was thinking that it's not always easy to warn people.'

44

I have said that I hate mysteries and I object on principle to hints and double meanings.

'When you want me to understand you, perhaps you will explain yourself more clearly,' I replied, rather brutally, perhaps, and I was sorry as soon as I had said it; for I saw her lips tremble a moment. She turned her head aside, then got up and took a few hesitating, almost tottering steps about the room.

'But, Amélie,' I cried, 'why do you go on being unhappy now that everything is all right again?' *because she knows it's not —*

I felt that my eyes embarrassed her, and it was with my back turned and my elbows on the table, resting my head in my hands, that I went on to say:

like wife in et fur

'I spoke to you unkindly just now. Forgive me.'

At that I heard her come up behind me; then I felt her lay her fingers gently on my head, as she said tenderly and in a voice trembling with tears:

know husband's

'My poor dear!' *she pities him.*
Then she left the room quickly.

heart is elsewhere.

Amélie's words, which I then thought so mysterious, became clear to me soon after this; I have written them down as they struck me at the moment; and that day I only understood that it was time Gertrude should leave.

He understands under

He's seen the danger

12 *March*

I had imposed on myself the duty of devoting a little time daily to Gertrude – a few hours or a few minutes, according to the occupations in hand. The day after this conversation with Amélie, I had some free time, and as the weather was inviting, I took Gertrude with me through the forest to that fold in the Jura where in the clear weather one can see, through a curtain of branches and across an immense stretch of land at one's feet, the wonder of the snowy Alps emerging from a thin veil of mist. The sun was already declining on the left when we reached our customary seat. A meadow of thick, closely cropped grass sloped downwards at our feet; further off, a few cows were grazing; each of them among these mountain herds wears a bell at its neck.

'They outline the landscape,' said Gertrude, as she listened to their tinkling.

She asked me, as she does every time we go for a walk, to describe the place where we had stopped.

'But you know it already,' I said; 'on the fringe of the forest, where one can see the Alps.'

'Can one see them clearly today?'

'Yes, in all their splendour.'

'You told me they were a little different every day.'

'What shall I compare them to this afternoon? To a thirsty midsummer's day. Before evening they will have melted into the air.'

'I should like you to tell me if there are any lilies in the big meadows before us?'

'No, Gertrude, lilies do not grow on these heights, or only a few rare species.'

'Not even the lilies called the lilies of the field?'

'There are no lilies in the fields.'

'Not even in the fields round about Neuchâtel?'

'There are no lilies of the field.'

'Then why did our Lord say "Look at the lilies of the field"?'

'There were some in His day, no doubt, for Him to say so; but they have disappeared before men and their ploughs.'

'I remember you have often told me that what this world most needs is confidence and love. Don't you think that with a little more confidence men would see them again? When I listen to His word, I assure you I see them. I will

46

she has great faith + is inspiring — attractive quality. sees everything through innocent, fresh eyes *her imagination is vivid & descriptive.*

describe them to you, shall I? They are like bells of flame –
great bells of azure, filled with the perfume of love and
swinging in the evening breeze. Why do you say there are
none there before us? I feel them. I see the meadow filled
with them.'

'They are not more beautiful than you see them, my
Gertrude.'

'Say they are not less beautiful.'

'They are as beautiful as you see them.'

'And yet I say unto you that even Solomon in all his
glory was not arrayed like one of these,' said she, quoting
Christ's words; and when I heard her melodious voice, I
felt I was listening to them for the first time. 'In all his
glory,' she repeated thoughtfully, and was silent for a time.
I went on:

'I have told you, Gertrude, that it is those who have eyes
who cannot see.' And a prayer rose from the bottom of my
heart: 'I thank Thee, O Lord, that Thou revealest to the
humble what Thou hidest from the wise.'

'If you knew,' she exclaimed in a rapture of delight, 'if
you knew how easily I imagine it all! Would you like me
to describe the landscape to you? ... Behind us, above us,
and around us are the great fir trees, with their scent of
resin and ruddy trunks, stretching out their long dark
horizontal branches and groaning as the wind tries to bend
them. At our feet, like an open book on the sloping desk of
the mountain, lies the broad green meadow, shot with shift-
ing colours – blue in the shade, golden in the sun, and
speaking in clear words of flowers – gentians, pulsatillas,
ranunculus and Solomon's beautiful lilies; the cows come
and spell them out with their bells; and the angels come
and read them – for you say that the eyes of men are closed.
Below the book I see a great smoky, misty river of milk,
hiding abysses of mystery – an immense river, whose only

47

*Vivid imagination – sees more
beauty than those who
can see.*

shore is the beautiful, dazzling Alps far, far away in the distance. . . . That's where Jacques is going. Tell me, is he really starting tomorrow?'

'He is to start tomorrow. Did he tell you so?'

'He didn't tell me so, but I guessed it. Will he be long away?'

'A month. . . . Gertrude, I want to ask you something. Why didn't you tell me that he used to meet you in the church?'

'He came twice. Oh, I don't want to hide anything from you; but I was afraid of making you unhappy.'

'It would make me unhappy if you didn't tell me.'

Her hand sought mine.

'He was sad at leaving.'

'Tell me, Gertrude . . . did he say he loved you?'

'He didn't say so, but I can feel it without being told. He doesn't love me as much as you do.'

'And you, Gertrude, does it make you unhappy that he should go away?'

'I think it is better he should go. I couldn't respond.'

'But tell me, does it make you unhappy that he should go?'

'You know, pastor, that it's you I love. . . . Oh, why do you take your hand away? I shouldn't speak so, if you weren't married. But no one marries a blind girl. Then why shouldn't we love one another? Tell me, pastor, do you think there's anything wrong in it?'

'It's never in love that the wrong lies.'

'I feel there is nothing but good in my heart. I don't want to make Jacques suffer. I don't want to make anyone suffer . . . I only want to give happiness.'

'Jacques was thinking of asking you to marry him.'

'Will you let me speak to him before he goes? I should like to make him understand that he must give up loving me. Pastor, you understand, don't you, that I can't marry anyone? You'll let me speak to him, won't you?'

'This evening.'

'No, tomorrow. Just before he leaves. . . .'

The sun was setting in majestic splendour. The evening air was warm. We had risen and, talking as we went, we turned back along the sombre homeward path.

25 April

I HAVE been obliged to put this book aside for some time. The snow melted at last and as soon as the roads were passable, there were a great many things to be done which I had been obliged to put off all the long while our village was isolated from the outer world. It was only yesterday I was able for the first time to find a few moments' leisure again.

Last night I read over everything I have written....

Now that I dare call by its name the feeling that so long lay unacknowledged in my heart, it seems almost incomprehensible that I should have mistaken it until this very day – incomprehensible that those words of Amélie's that I recorded here should have appeared mysterious – that even after Gertrude's naïve declarations I should still have doubted that I loved her. The fact is that I would not then allow that any love outside marriage could be permissible, nor at the same time would I allow that there could be anything whatever forbidden in the feeling that drew me so passionately to Gertrude.

The innocence of her avowals, their very frankness reassured me. I told myself she was only a child. Real love would not go without confusion and blushes. As far as I was concerned, I persuaded myself I loved her as one loves an afflicted child. I tended her as one tends a sick person – and so I made a moral obligation, a duty of what was really a passionate inclination. Yes truly, on the very evening she spoke to me in the way I have described, so happy was I, so light of heart that I misunderstood my real feelings and even as I transcribed our talk, I misunderstood them still.

For I should have considered love reprehensible, and my conviction was that everything reprehensible must lie heavy on the soul; therefore, as I felt no weight on my soul, I had no thought of love.

These conversations were set down not only just as they occurred, but were also written while I was in the same frame of mind as when they took place; to tell the truth, it was only when I re-read them last night that I understood. ... *another revelation – that it's not love one has 4 a child.*

As soon as Jacques had gone (I had allowed Gertrude to speak to him before he left, and when he returned for the last few days of the holidays, he affected either to avoid her altogether or to speak to her only in my presence) our life slipped back into its usual peaceful course. Gertrude, as had been arranged, went to stay at Mlle Louise's, where I visited her every day. But, again in my fear of love, I made a point of not talking to her of anything likely to agitate us. I spoke to her only as a pastor and for the most part in Louise's presence, occupying myself chiefly with her religious instruction and preparing her for Holy Communion, which she has just partaken of this Easter. *he's trying against the feeling*

I too communicated on Easter Day.

This was a fortnight ago. To my surprise Jacques, who was spending a week's holiday with us, did not accompany us to the Lord's Table. And I greatly regret having to say that Amélie also abstained – for the first time since our marriage. It seemed as though the two of them had come to an understanding and resolved by their abstention from this solemn celebration to throw a shadow over my joy. Here again I congratulated myself that Gertrude could not see and that I was left to bear the weight of this shadow alone. I know Amélie too well not to be aware of all the blame she wished indirectly to convey by her conduct. She never *he's driving them away*

51

She can see more than you think

openly disapproves of me, but she makes a point of showing her displeasure by leaving me in a sort of isolation.

I was profoundly distressed that a grievance of this kind — such a one, I mean, as I shrink from contemplating — should have so affected Amélie's soul as to turn her aside from her higher interests. And when I came home I prayed for her in all sincerity of heart.

As for Jacques' abstention, it was due to quite another motive, as I learnt from a conversation I had with him a little later on.

3 May

Gertrude's religious instruction has led me to re-read the Gospels with a fresh eye. It seems to me more and more that many of the notions that constitute our Christian faith originate not from Christ's own words but from St Paul's commentaries.

This was, in fact, the subject of the discussion I have just had with Jacques. By disposition he is somewhat hard and rigid, and his mind is not sufficiently nourished by his heart; he is becoming traditionalist and dogmatic. He reproaches me with choosing out of the Christian doctrine 'what pleases me'. But I do not pick and choose among Christ's words. I simply, between Christ and St Paul, choose Christ. He, on the contrary, for fear of finding them in opposition, refuses to dissociate them, refuses to feel any difference of inspiration between them, and makes objections when I say that in one case it is a man I hear, while in the other it is God. The more he argues, the more persuaded I am he does not feel that Christ's slightest word has a divine accent that is unique.

I search the Gospels, I search in vain for commands, threats, prohibitions. . . . All of these come from St Paul. And it is precisely because they are not to be found in the words of Christ that Jacques is disturbed. Souls like his think themselves lost as soon as they are deprived of their props, their hand-rails, their fences. And besides, they cannot endure others to enjoy a liberty they have resigned, and want to obtain by compulsion what would readily be granted by love.

'But, Father,' he said, 'I too desire the soul's happiness.'

'No, my friend, you desire its submission.'

I leave him the last word because I dislike arguing; but I know that happiness is endangered when one seeks to obtain it by what should on the contrary be the effect of happiness – and if it is true that the loving soul rejoices in a willing submission, nothing is further from happiness than submission without love.

For the rest Jacques reasons well, and if I were not distressed at seeing so much doctrinal harshness in so young a mind, I should no doubt admire the quality of his arguments and his unbending logic. It often seems to me that I am younger than he is – younger today than I was yesterday – and I repeat to myself the words:

'Except ye become as little children, ye shall not enter into the kingdom of Heaven.'

Do I betray Christ, do I slight, do I profane the Gospels when I see in them above all a *method for attaining the life of blessedness?* The state of joy, which doubt and the hardness of our hearts alone prevent, is an obligation laid upon every Christian. Every living creature is more or less capable of joy. Every living creature ought to tend to joy. Gertrude's smile alone teaches me more in this respect than all my lessons teach her.

And these words of Christ's stood out before my eyes in letters of light: 'If ye were blind ye should have no sin.' Sin is that which darkens the soul – which prevents its joy. Gertrude's perfect happiness, which shines forth from her whole being, comes from the fact that she does not know sin. There is nothing in her but light and love.

I have put into her vigilant hands the four Gospels, the Psalms, the Apocalypse, and the three Epistles of St John, so that she may read, 'God is light, and in Him is no darkness at all,' as in the Gospel she has already heard the Saviour say, 'I am the light of the world.' I will not give her the Epistles of St Paul, for if, being blind, she knows not sin, what is the use of troubling her by letting her read, 'sin by the commandment might become exceeding sinful' (Romans vii. 13) and the whole of the dialectic that follows, admirable as it may be.

8 May

Dr Martins came over yesterday from Chaux-de-Fonds. He examined Gertrude's eyes for a long time with the ophthalmoscope. He told me he had spoken to Dr Roux, the Lausanne specialist, about her and is to report his observations to him. They both have an idea that Gertrude might be operated on with success. But we have agreed to say nothing about it to her as long as things are not more certain. Martins is to come and let me know what they think after they have consulted. What would be the good of raising Gertrude's hopes if there is any risk of their being immediately extinguished? And besides, is she not happy as she is? ...

10 May

At Easter Jacques and Gertrude saw each other again in my presence – at least, Jacques had a visit from Gertrude and spoke to her, only about trifles, however. He seemed less agitated than I feared; and I persuade myself afresh that if his love had really been very ardent, he would not have got over it so easily, even though Gertrude had told him last year before he went away that it was hopeless.

I notice that he no longer says 'thou' to Gertrude but calls her 'you', which is certainly preferable; however, I had not asked him to do so and I am glad it was his own idea. There is undoubtedly a great deal of good in him.

I suspect, however, that this submission of Jacques' was not arrived at without a struggle. The unfortunate thing is that the constraint he has been obliged to impose on his feelings now seems to him good in itself; he would like to see it imposed on everyone; I felt this in the discussion I had with him which I have recorded further back. Is it not La Rochefoucauld who says that the mind is often the dupe of the heart? I need not say that, knowing Jacques as I do, I did not venture to point this out to him there and then, for I take him to be one of those people who are only made more obstinate by argument; but the very same evening I looked out what furnished me with a reply – and from St Paul himself (I could only beat him with his own weapons) – and left a little note in his room, in which I wrote out the text, 'Let not him that eateth despise him that eateth not: for God hath received him' (Romans xiv. 3).

I might as well have copied out what follows: 'I know, and am persuaded by the Lord Jesus, that there is nothing unclean of itself: but to him that esteemeth anything to be unclean, to him it is unclean.' – But I did not dare to, for I was afraid that Jacques might proceed to suspect me of some wrongful interpretation with regard to Gertrude – a suspicion which must not so much as cross his imagination for a second. Evidently it is here a question of food; but in how many passages of the Scriptures are we not called on to give the words a double and triple meaning? ('If thine eye' ... the multiplication of the loaves; the miracle of Cana, etc. ...) This is not a matter of logic-chopping; the meaning of this text is wide and deep: the restriction must not be dictated by the law but by love, and St Paul exclaims immediately afterwards: 'But if thy brother be grieved with

55

thy meat, now walkest thou not charitably.' It is where love fails that the chink in our armour lies. That is where the Evil One attacks us. Lord, remove from my heart all that does not belong to love. ... For I was wrong to provoke Jacques: the next morning I found on my table the same note on which I had written out the text; Jacques had simply written on the back of it another text from the same chapter: 'Destroy not him with thy meat, for whom Christ died' (Romans xiv. 15).

I have re-read the whole chapter. It is the starting-point for endless discussion. And is Gertrude to be tormented with these perplexities? Is the brightness of her sky to be darkened with these clouds? Am I not nearer Christ, do I not keep her nearer to Him, when I teach her, when I let her believe that the only sin is that which hurts the happiness of others or endangers our own?

Alas! there are some souls to whom happiness is uncongenial; they cannot, they do not know how to avail themselves of it. ... I am thinking of my poor Amélie. I never cease imploring her, urging her – I wish I could force her to be happy. Yes, I wish I could lift everyone among us up to God. But she will none of it; she curls up like certain flowers which never open to the sun. Everything she sees causes her uneasiness and distress.

'What's the good, my dear?' she answered me the other day; 'we can't all be blind.'

Ah, how her irony grieves me! And what courage I need not to be disturbed by it! And yet it seems to me she ought to understand that this allusion to Gertrude's infirmity is particularly painful to me. She makes me feel, indeed, that what I admire above all in Gertrude is her infinite mildness; I have never heard her express the slightest resentment against anyone. It is true I do not allow her to hear anything that might hurt her.

protective dher – 56
fatherly rightly – compares
her with daughter Charlotte

And as the soul that is happy diffuses happiness around
it by the radiation of love, so everything in Amélie's neighbourhood becomes gloomy and morose. Amiel would say
that her soul gives out black rays. When, after a harassing
day of toil – visits to the sick, the poor, the afflicted – I come
in at nightfall, tired out and with a heart longing for rest,
affection, warmth, it is to find, more often than not,
worries, recriminations and quarrels, which I dread a
thousand times more than the cold, the wind and the rain
out of doors. I know well enough that our old Rosalie in-
variably wants her own way, but she is not always in the
wrong! nor Amélie always in the right when she tries to
make her give in. I know that Gaspard and Charlotte are
horribly unruly; but would not Amélie get better results if
she scolded them less loudly and less constantly? So much
nagging, so many reprimands and expostulations lose their
edge like pebbles on the seashore; they are far less disturbing to the children than to me. I know that Claude is teeth-
ing (at least that is what his mother declares every time he
sets up a howl), but does it not encourage him to howl, for
her or Sarah to run and pick him up and be for ever petting
him? I am convinced he would not howl so often if he was
left to howl once or twice to his heart's content when I am
not there. But I know that is the very time they spoil him
most.

Sarah is like her mother, and for that reason I should
have wished to send her to school. She is not, alas, what
her mother was at her age when we were first engaged, but
what the material cares of life have made her – I was going
to say the *cultivation* of the cares of life, for Amélie certainly
does cultivate them. I find it indeed very difficult to recognize in her today the angel of those early times, who
smiled encouragement on every high-minded impulse of
my heart, who I dreamt would be the sharer of my every

57

lost what they had.
Life has hardened her
made her sceptical.

his family is not interesting
enough — he prefers his own comp.

LA SYMPHONIE PASTORALE

hope and fear, and whom I looked on as my guide and
leader along the path to Heaven – or did love blind me in
those days? ... I cannot see that Sarah has any interests
that are not vulgar; like her mother, she allows herself to
be entirely taken up with paltry household matters; the very
features of her face, unilluminated as they are by any
inward flame, look dull and almost hard. She has no taste
for poetry or for reading in general; I never overhear any
conversation between her and her mother in which I have
any inclination to take part, and I feel my isolation even
more painfully when I am with them than when I retire to
my study, as it is becoming my custom to do more and more
often.

And I have also fallen into the habit this autumn –
encouraged by the shortness of the days – of taking tea at
Mlle de la M ...'s whenever my rounds permit it, that is
whenever I can get back early enough. I have not yet
mentioned that since last November Mlle de la M ... has
extended her hospitality to three little blind girls, entrusted
to her care by Martins. Gertrude is teaching them to read
and to work at sundry little tasks over which they have
already begun to be quite clever.

How restful, how comforting I find its warm friendly
atmosphere every time I re-enter the Grange, and how
much I miss it if I am obliged to let two or three days pass
without going there. Mlle de la M ..., it is hardly necessary
to say, has sufficient means to take in and provide for
Gertrude and the three little boarders without putting herself out in any way; three maid-servants help her with the
greatest devotion and save her all fatigue. Can one imagine
fortune and leisure better bestowed? Louise de la M ... has
always interested herself in the poor; she is a profoundly
religious woman and seems hardly to belong to this earth
or to live for anything but love; though her hair is already

silvery under its lace cap, nothing can be more childlike
than her laugh, nothing more harmonious than her movements, nothing more musical than her voice. Gertrude has
caught her manners, her way of speaking, almost the in-
tonation, not only of her voice, but of her mind, of her
whole being – a likeness upon which I tease them both, but
which neither of them will admit. How sweet it is, when I
can find the time, to linger in their company, to see them
sitting beside each other, Gertrude either leaning her head
on her friend's shoulder, or clasping one of her hands in
hers, while I read them some lines out of Lamartine or
Hugo; how sweet to behold the beauties of such poetry
reflected in the mirror of their limpid souls! Even the little
pupils are touched by it. These children, in this atmosphere
of peace and love, develop astonishingly and their progress
is wonderful. I smiled at first when Mlle Louise spoke of
teaching them to dance – for their health's sake as much
as for their amusement; but now I admire the rhythmic
grace to which they have attained, though they themselves,
alas, are unable to appreciate it. And yet Louise de la M ...
has persuaded me that though they cannot see, they do
physically perceive the harmony of their movements. Gertrude takes part in their dances with the most charming
grace and sweetness, and moreover seems to take the keen-
est pleasure in them. Or sometimes it is Louise de la M ...
who directs the little girls' movements, and then Gertrude
seats herself at the piano. Her progress in music is astonish-
ing; she plays the organ in chapel now every Sunday. Every
Sunday she comes to lunch with us; my children are delighted to see her, notwithstanding that their tastes are
growing more and more divergent. Amélie is not too irrit-
able and we get through the meal without a hitch. After
lunch, the whole family goes back with Gertrude to the
Grange and has tea there. It is a treat for my children and

59

Louise enjoys spoiling them and loading them with cakes and sweetmeats. Amélie, who is far from being insensible to attentions of this kind, unbends at last and looks ten years younger. I think she would find it difficult now to do without this halt in the wearisome round of her daily life.

18 May

Now that the fine weather has returned, I have been able to go out again with Gertrude – a thing I had not done for a long time (for there have been fresh falls of snow quite recently and the roads have been in a terrible state until only a few days ago), and it is a long time too since I have found myself alone with her.

We walked quickly; the sharp air coloured her cheeks and kept blowing her fair hair over her face. As we passed alongside a peat-moss, I picked one or two rushes that were in flower and slipped their stalks under her béret; then I twined them into her hair so as to keep them in place.

We had scarcely spoken to each other as yet in the astonishment of finding ourselves alone together, when Gertrude turned her sightless face towards me and asked abruptly:

'Do you think Jacques still loves me?'

'He has made up his mind to give you up,' I replied at once.

'But do you think he knows you love me?' she went on.

Since the conversation which I have related above, more than six months had gone by without (strange to say) the slightest word of love having passed between us. We were never alone, as I have said, and it was better so. .... Gertrude's question made my heart beat so fast that I was obliged to slacken our pace a little.

'My dear Gertrude, everyone knows I love you,' I cried. But she was not to be put off.

'No, no; you have not answered my question.'

60

And after a moment's silence, she went on with lowered head:

'Aunt Amélie knows it; and *I* know it makes her sad.'

'She would be sad anyway,' I protested with an unsteady voice; 'it is her nature to be sad.'

'Oh, you always try to reassure me,' she answered with some impatience. 'But I don't want to be reassured. There are a great many things, I feel sure, you don't tell me about for fear of troubling or grieving me; a great many things I don't know, so that sometimes . . .'

Her voice dropped lower and lower; she stopped as if for want of breath. And when, taking up her last words, I asked:

'So that sometimes? . . .'

'So that sometimes,' she continued sadly, 'I think all the happiness I owe you is founded upon ignorance.'

'But, Gertrude . . .'

'No, let me say this – I don't want a happiness of that kind. You must understand that I don't . . . I don't care about being happy. I would rather know. There are a great many things – sad things assuredly – that I can't see, but you have no right to keep them from me. I have reflected a great deal during these last winter months; I am afraid, you know, that the whole world is not as beautiful as you have made out, pastor – and in fact, that it is very far from it.'

'It is true that man has often defaced it,' I argued timidly, for the rush of her thoughts frightened me and I tried to turn it aside, though without daring to hope I should succeed. She seemed to be waiting for these words, for she seized on them at once as though they were the missing link in the chain:

'Exactly!' she cried; 'I want to be sure of not adding to the evil.'

61

For a long time we walked on very quickly and in silence. Everything I might have said was checked beforehand by what I felt she was thinking; I dreaded to provoke some sentence which might set both our fates trembling in the balance. And as I thought of what Martins had said as to the possibility of her regaining her sight, a dreadful anxiety gripped me.

'I wanted to ask you,' she went on at last ' – but I don't know how to say it. . . .'

Certainly she needed all her courage to speak, just as I needed all mine to listen. But how could I have foreseen the question that was tormenting her?

'Are the children of a blind woman always born blind?'

'No, Gertrude,' I said, 'except in very special cases. There is, in fact, no reason why they should be.'

She seemed extremely reassured. I should have liked in my turn to ask her why she wanted to know this; I had not the courage and went on clumsily:

'But, Gertrude, to have children one must be married.'

'Don't tell me that, pastor, I know it's not true.'

'I have told you what it was proper for me to tell you,' I protested. 'But it is true, the laws of nature do allow what is forbidden by the laws of man and God.'

'You have often told me the laws of God were the laws of love.'

'But such love as that is not the same that also goes by the name of Charity.'

'Is it out of Charity you love me?'

'No, my Gertrude, you know it is not.'

'Then you admit our love is outside the laws of God?'

'What do you mean?'

'Oh, you know well enough, and I ought not to be the one to say so.'

I sought in vain for some way of evasion; the beating of my heart set all my arguments flying in confusion.

'Gertrude,' I exclaimed wildly, '. . . you think your love wrong?'

She corrected me:

'*Our love* . . . I say to myself I ought to think so.'

'And then? . . .'

I heard what sounded like a note of supplication in my voice, while without waiting to take breath, she went on:

'But that I cannot stop loving you.'   *she's beginning to think it's wrong*

All this happened yesterday. I hesitated at first to write it down. . . . I have no idea how our walk came to an end. We hurried along as if we were being pursued, while I held her arm tightly pressed against me. My soul was so absent from my body that I felt as if the smallest pebble in the path might send us both rolling to the ground.

19 May

Martins came back this morning. Gertrude's is a case for operation. Roux is certain of it and wishes to have her under his care for a time. I cannot refuse and yet, such is my cowardice that I asked to be allowed to reflect. I asked to have time to prepare her gently. . . . My heart should leap for joy, but it feels inexpressibly heavy, weighed down by a sick misgiving. At the thought of having to tell Gertrude her sight may be restored to her, my heart fails me altogether.   *is he scared at what she'll think upon she sees him —*

19 May. Night

I have seen Gertrude and I have not told her. At the Grange this evening there was no one in the drawing-room; I went upstairs to her room. We were alone.

I held her long in my arms pressed to my heart. She made no attempt to resist, and as she raised her face to mine our lips met. . . .

that time anything happened

Or that she'll lose her innocence to the world the world

63

21 May

O Lord, is it for us Thou has clothed the night with such depth and beauty? Is it for me? The air is warm and the moon shines in at my open window as I sit listening to the vast silence of the skies. Oh, from all creation rises a blended adoration which bears my heart along, lost in an ecstasy that knows no words. I cannot – I cannot pray with calm. If there is any limitation to love, it is set by man and not by Thee, my God. However guilty my love may appear in the eyes of men, oh, tell me that in Thine, it is sacred.

I try to rise above the idea of sin; but sin seems to me intolerable, and I will not give up Christ. No, I will not admit that I sin in loving Gertrude. I could only succeed in tearing this love from my heart if I tore my heart out with it, and for what? If I did not already love her, it would be my duty to love her for pity's sake; to cease to love her would be to betray her; she needs my love. . . .

Lord, I know not . . . I know nothing now but Thee. Be Thou my guide. Sometimes I feel that darkness is closing round me and that it is I who have been deprived of the sight that is to be restored to her. *It is as if he has gone spiritually blind.*

Gertrude went into the Lausanne nursing-home yesterday and is not to come out for three weeks. I am expecting her return with extreme apprehension. Martins is to bring her back. She has made me promise not to try to see her before then.

22 May

A letter from Martins: the operation has been successful. God be thanked!

24 May

The idea that she who loved me without seeing me must now see me causes me intolerable discomfort. Will she know me? For the first time in my life I consult the mirror. If I feel her eyes are less indulgent than her heart and less loving, what will become of me? O Lord, I sometimes think I have need of her love in order to love Thee!

8 June

An unusual amount of work has enabled me to get through these last days with tolerable patience. Every occupation that takes me out of myself is a merciful one; but all day long and through all that happens her image is with me.

She is coming back tomorrow. Amélie, who during these last weeks has shown only the best side of herself and seems endeavouring to distract my thoughts, is preparing a little festivity with the children to welcome her return.

9 June

Gaspard and Charlotte have picked what flowers they could find in the woods and fields. Old Rosalie has manufactured a monumental cake which Sarah is decorating with gold paper ornaments. We are expecting her this morning for lunch. I am writing to fill in the time of waiting. It is eleven o'clock. Every moment I raise my head and look out at the road along which Martins's carriage will come. I resist the temptation to go and meet them; it is better – especially for Amélie's sake — that I should not welcome her apart from the others. My heart leaps. . . . Ah! Here they are!

9 June. Evening

Oh, in what abominable darkness I am plunged.

Pity, Lord, pity! I renounce loving her, but do Thou not let her die.

How right my fears were! What has she done? What did she want to do? Amélie and Sarah tell me they went with her as far as the door of the Grange, where Mlle de la M . . . was expecting her. So she must have gone out again. . . . What happened?

I try to put my thoughts into some sort of order. The accounts they give are incomprehensible or contradictory. My mind is utterly confused. ... Mlle de la M ...'s gardener has just brought her back to the Grange unconscious; he says he saw her walking by the river, then she crossed the garden bridge, then stooped and disappeared; but as he did not at first realize that she had fallen, he did not run to her help as he should have done; he found her at the little sluice, where she had been carried by the stream. When I saw her soon afterwards she had not recovered consciousness; or at least had lost it again, for she came to for a moment, thanks to the prompt measures that were taken. Martins, who, thank Heaven, had not yet left, cannot understand the kind of stupor and lassitude in which she is now sunk. He has questioned her in vain; she seems either not to hear or else to be determined not to speak. Her breathing is very laboured and Martins is afraid of pneumonia; he has ordered sinapisms and cupping and has promised to come again tomorrow. The mistake was leaving her too long in her wet clothes while they were trying to bring her round; the water of the river is icy. Mlle de la M ..., who is the only person who has succeeded in getting a few words from her, declares she wanted to pick some of the forget-me-nots that grow in abundance on this side of the river, and that being still unaccustomed to measure distances or else mistaking the floating carpet of flowers for solid ground, she suddenly lost her footing. ... If I could only believe it! If I could only persuade myself it was nothing but an accident, what a dreadful load would be lifted from my heart! During the whole meal, though it was so gay, the strange smile that never left her face made me uneasy; a forced smile, which I had never seen her wear before, but which I tried my utmost to believe was the smile of her newly born sight; a smile which seemed to stream from her eyes

66

she's changed – realising her mistake + feeling shame

on to her face like tears, and beside which the vulgar mirth of the others seemed offensive. She did not join in the mirth; I felt as if she had discovered a secret she would surely have confided to me if we had been alone. She hardly spoke; but no one was surprised at that, because she is often silent when she is with others and all the more so when their merriment grows noisy.

Lord, I beseech Thee, let me speak to her. I must know, or how can I continue to live? ... And yet if she really wished to end her life, is it just because she *knew?* Knew what? Dear, what horrible thing can you have learnt? What did I hide from you that was so deadly? What can you so suddenly have seen?

I have been spending two hours at her bedside, my eyes never leaving her forehead, her pale cheeks, her delicate eyelids, shut down over some unspeakable sorrow, her hair still wet and like seaweed as it lies spread round about her on the pillow – listening to her difficult, irregular breathing.

10 June

Mlle Louise sent for me this morning just as I was starting to go to the Grange. After a fairly quiet night, Gertrude has at last emerged from her torpor. She smiled when I went into the room and signed to me to come and sit by her bedside. I did not dare question her, and no doubt she was dreading my questions, for she said immediately, as though to forestall anything emotional:

'What do you call those little blue flowers that I wanted to pick up by the river? Flowers the colour of the sky? Will you be cleverer than I and pick me a bunch of them? I should like to have them here beside my bed. ...'

The false cheerfulness of her voice was dreadful to me; and no doubt she was aware of it, for she added more gravely:

pushing him away

'I can't speak to you this morning; I am too tired. Go and pick those flowers for me, will you? You can come back again later.'

And when, an hour later, I brought her the bunch of forget-me-nots, Mlle Louise told me that Gertrude was resting and could not see me before evening.

I saw her again this evening. She was lying – almost sitting up in bed – propped against a pile of pillows. Her hair was now fastened up, with the forget-me-nots I had brought her twisted into the plaits above her forehead.

She was obviously very feverish and drew her breath with great difficulty. She kept the hand I put out to her in her burning hand; I remained standing beside her:

'I must confess something to you, pastor; because this evening I am afraid of dying,' she said. 'What I told you this morning was a lie. It was not to pick flowers ... Will you forgive me if I say I wanted to kill myself?'

I fell on my knees beside the bed, still keeping her frail hand in mine; but she disengaged it and began to stroke my head, while I buried my face in the sheets so as to hide my tears and stifle my sobs.

'Do you think it was very wrong?' she went on tenderly; then, as I answered nothing:

'My friend, my friend,' she said, 'you must see that I take up too much room in your heart and in your life. When I came back to you, that was what struck me at once – or at any rate, that the place I took belonged to another and that it made her unhappy. My crime is that I did not feel it sooner; or rather – for indeed I knew it all along – that I allowed you to love me in spite of it. But when her face suddenly appeared to – when I saw such unhappiness on her poor face, I could not bear the idea that that unhappiness was my work. ... No, no, don't blame yourself for anything; but let me go, and give her back her joy.'

feels guilt

Now she can see, she saw the grief on Amelie's face + realised what their love has done – feels guilt.

The hand ceased stroking my head; I seized it and covered it with kisses and tears. But she drew it away impatiently and began to toss in the throes of some fresh emotion.

'That is not what I wanted to say to you; no, it's not that I wanted to say,' she kept repeating, and I saw the sweat on her damp forehead. Then she closed her eyes and kept them shut for a time, as though to concentrate her thoughts or to recover her former state of blindness; and in a voice which at first was trailing and mournful, but which soon, as she reopened her eyes, grew louder, grew at last animated even to vehemence:

'When you gave me back my sight,' she began, 'my eyes opened on a world more beautiful than I had ever dreamt it could be; yes truly, I had never imagined the daylight so bright, the air so brilliant, the sky so vast. But I had never imagined men's faces so full of care either: and when I went into your house, do you know what it was that struck me first? ... Oh, it can't be helped, I must tell you: what I saw first of all was our fault, our sin. No, don't protest. You remember Christ's words, "If ye were blind ye should have no sin." But now I see ... Get up, pastor. Sit there, beside me. Listen to me without interrupting. During the time I spent in the nursing-home, I read – or rather I had read to me some verses of the Bible I did not know – some you had never read to me. I remember a text of St Paul's which I repeated to myself all one day. "For I was alive without the law once; but when the commandment came, sin revived and I died."'

She spoke in a state of extreme excitement and in a very loud voice, almost shouting the last words, so that I was made uncomfortable by the idea that they might be heard outside the room; then she shut her eyes and repeated in a whisper as though for herself alone:

'Sin revived – and I died.'

I shivered and my heart froze in a kind of terror. I tried to turn aside her thoughts:

'Who read you those texts?' I asked.

'Jacques,' she said, opening her eyes and looking at me fixedly. 'Did you know he was converted?'

It was more than I could bear; I was going to implore her to stop, but she had already gone on:

'My friend, I am going to grieve you very much; but there must be no falsehood between us now. When I saw Jacques, I suddenly realized it was not you I loved – but him. He had your face – I mean the face I imagined you had ... Ah! why did you make me refuse him? I might have married him. ...'

blaming him again

'But, Gertrude, you still can,' I cried with despair in my heart.

'He is entering the priesthood,' she said impetuously. Then, shaken by sobs, 'Oh, I want to confess to him,' she moaned in a kind of ecstasy. ... 'You see for yourself, there's nothing left me but to die. I am thirsty. Please call someone. I can't breathe. Leave me. I want to be alone. Ah! I had hoped that speaking to you would have brought me more relief. You must say good-bye. We must say good-bye. I cannot bear to be with you any more.'

ends in tragedy as she resents him now

I left her. I called Mlle de la M ... to take my place beside her; her extreme agitation made me fear the worst, but I could not help seeing that my presence did her harm. I begged that I might be sent for if there was a change for the worse.

11 June

Alas! I was never to see her again alive. She died this morning after a night of delirium and exhaustion. Jacques, who at Gertrude's dying request was telegraphed for by Mlle de la M ..., arrived a few hours after the end. He reproached me cruelly for not having called in a priest

[handwritten at top: + selfish — He has been morally blind + it has ended in death]

while there was yet time. But how could I have done so, when I was still unaware that during her stay at Lausanne, and evidently urged by him, Gertrude had abjured the Protestant faith? He told me in the same breath of his own conversion and Gertrude's. And so they both left me at the same time; it seemed as if, separated by me during their lifetime, they had planned to escape me here and be united to each other in God. But I tell myself that Jacques' conversion is more a matter of the head than the heart.

[handwritten right margin: had realised what he had kept from them.]

'Father,' he said, 'it is not fitting for me to make accusations against you; but it was the example of your error that guided me.'

After Jacques had left again, I knelt down beside Amélie and asked her to pray for me, as I was in need of help. She simply repeated 'Our Father . . .' but between each sentence she left long pauses which we filled with our supplication.

I would have wept, but I felt my heart more arid than the desert.

[handwritten: empty, emotionless, unable to live.]

ISABELLE

To André Ruyters

ISABELLE

GÉRARD LACASE, with whom Francis Jammes and myself were staying in the August of 189—, took us one day to see the château of La Quartfourche, which even then was hardly more than a ruin. It stood in a great deserted park where summer was lavishing its glories with unrestrained prodigality. Nothing remained to forbid intrusion —neither the half-filled boundary ditch, nor the broken-down hedges, nor the iron park gates, which hung on loosened hinges and yielded crazily to our first push. No trace of paths was left; a few cows had been let loose to graze on the unkempt luxuriant grass of the overgrown lawns, and others were seeking shelter from the sun in the cool hollows now gutted of their trees; in the midst of this wild profusion it was only here and there that some flower or rare foliage could be distinguished — patient remnants of former cultivation, but now almost smothered out of existence by the invasion of more vulgar species. We followed Gérard without speaking, oppressed by the beauty of the place, the season, and the hour, and feeling, too, all the neglect and heart-ache that perhaps lay hidden under this excessive opulence. The perron — the lower steps of which were swamped in grass and the upper cracked and disjointed — was soon reached; but when we tried to get into the drawing-room, the barred shutters of the french windows stopped us. We entered the house at last like thieves, by crawling through one of the cellar lights; a flight of steps led up to the kitchens; not one of the inside doors was shut ... and as we passed from room to room — walking warily, for the sagging floors looked as if they might give way beneath us at any moment

– we stifled the sound of our steps, not that we thought there was anyone to hear them, but because the noise of our presence re-echoing through the profound silence of the empty house sounded unseemly and almost alarming. Several panes were missing in the ground-floor windows and a begonia had thrust its huge, white, flabby stalks through the slats of the shutters into the dusky half-light of the dining-room.

Gérard had left us; he had known the former owners of the house and we thought he might prefer to revisit the place alone, so we continued our inspection without him. No doubt he had gone up to the first floor and passed before us through the bare and desolate rooms; in one of them a small branch of box was still hanging on the wall from a kind of hook to which it was tied by a bit of faded ribbon; it seemed to be swinging slightly at the end of its loop, and I thought to myself that Gérard must just have pulled a twig from it as he passed by.

We came across him again in a passage on the second floor. There was no glass in the window beside which he was standing, and a dangling rope had been pulled through it from the outside; it was a bell-rope, and I was on the point of giving it a gentle pull when I felt Gérard seize my arm; his action, instead of stopping mine, only accentuated it: a hoarse clang suddenly rang out; it sounded so near us and so harsh that it made us start; then, when silence seemed to have quite closed in again, one more note and after it another dropped slowly down, pure and distant. I looked at Gérard and saw his lips were trembling.

'Let us come away,' he said; 'I can't breathe here.'

As soon as we were outside, he excused himself for leaving us; there was someone in the neighbourhood he wanted to inquire after. We understood from his tone of voice that it would be indiscreet to follow him, so Jammes and I returned alone to La R., where he joined us in the course of the evening.

'My dear fellow,' said Jammes after a time, 'let me warn you that I am determined not to tell you the smallest tale until you come out with the one you obviously have on your mind.'

Now Jammes' tales were the delight of our evenings.

'I would willingly tell you the story the scene of which was laid in the house you saw this afternoon,' began Gérard, 'but I was only able to discover or reconstruct it partially; besides which I am afraid that if I attempt to tell it you in any sort of order, I shall strip it of all the attraction of baffling mystery with which my curiosity invested each event as it occurred.'

'Put as little order into your story as you please,' said Jammes.

'Why should one try to rearrange facts in their chronological sequence?' added I. 'Why not put them before us just as you discovered them?'

'Then you must allow me to talk a great deal about myself.'

'Which of us ever does anything else?' was Jammes' rejoinder.

This is the story Gérard told us.

CHAPTER ONE

I CAN hardly understand nowadays the impatience with which I then flung myself upon life. At twenty-five years of age I knew almost nothing of it except from books; and that no doubt is why I thought myself a novelist; for I had not as yet realized how cunningly and maliciously events conceal from us just that part of themselves most likely to interest us, and how slight a handle they offer the man who is incapable of wresting their secret from them by force.

I was at that time preparing a thesis on the chronology of Bossuet's sermons, with a view to my doctor's degree; not that I was particularly attracted by pulpit oratory; I had chosen the subject out of deference to my old master, Albert Desnos, who had just completed the publication of his great Life of Bossuet. As soon as Monsieur Desnos heard of my plans, he offered to assist me in gaining access to the material. One of his oldest friends, Benjamin Floche, of the Académie des Inscriptions et Belles Lettres, possessed various documents which would no doubt be of use to me, and in particular a Bible covered with annotations in Bossuet's own handwriting. Monsieur Floche, who had retired to the country about fifteen years earlier, was living at a place called La Quartfourche, more commonly known as Le Carrefour or the Crossways, an old family estate in the neighbourhood of Pont-l'Évêque, from which he never stirred and where he would be delighted to receive me and put at my service his papers, his library, and his learning – which Monsieur Desnos said was inexhaustible.

Letters were exchanged between Monsieur Desnos and Monsieur Floche. The documents, it appeared, were more numerous than my master had at first led me to expect; there was soon no question of a mere afternoon's visit; Monsieur Floche was kind enough, on the recommendation of Monsieur Desnos, to invite me to stay for a while at the château of La Quartfourche. Although Monsieur and Madame Floche had no children, they did not live alone; a few careless words let fall by Monsieur Desnos fired my imagination and filled me with the hope of meeting company there far more attractive than any dusty documents of the seventeenth century; my thesis soon became a mere pretext; it was no longer as a scholar that I proposed to visit the château, but as a Nejdanof,* as a Valmont;† I peopled it with adventures. La Quartfourche! The Crossways! I repeated the mysterious name again and again. 'This,' thought I, 'is the scene of Hercules' hesitation ... I know indeed what awaits him on the path of virtue; but what of the other road? ... the other road. ...'

Towards the middle of September I put together the best of my modest wardrobe, replenished my selection of ties, and started.

When I reached the station of Breuil-Blangy, between Pont-l'Évêque and Lisieux, it was already night. I was the only person to get out of the train. A sort of peasant dressed in livery came up to me, took my bag, and escorted me to the carriage that was waiting on the other side of the station. The appearance of the horse and carriage cut short any flights of imagination. A more lamentable turn-out cannot be conceived. The peasant coachman went to fetch my trunk, which I had registered, and the springs of the old barouche sank under its weight. Inside there was a suffocating smell of poultry; ... I tried to let down the window, and the strap came off in my hand. There had been rain during

---

*Nejdanof, hero of *Virgin Soil* by Turgenev.

†Valmont, hero of *Les Liaisons dangereuses* by Laclos.

the day and the roads were heavy; at the bottom of the first hill a part of the harness gave way. The coachman pulled a bit of string from under the seat and set to work doctoring the trace. I had got out of the carriage and offered to hold the carriage lamp for him; I could see that the poor man's livery, like the harness, had more than once been in need of patching.

'The leather is a bit old,' I hazarded.

He looked at me as if I had insulted him and answered almost brutally:

'It was lucky for you, mister, we were able to fetch you.'

'Is the château far?' I asked in my gentlest voice. He made no direct answer to my question, but:

'You may be sure it's not a journey we do every day!' he growled.

Then, after a moment:

'It's a matter of six months maybe that the carriage hasn't been out. . . .'

'Oh! Your masters don't go driving often?' I went on, in a desperate effort to keep the conversation going.

'No, indeed! As if there weren't other things to do!'

The damage was repaired by now and he motioned me to get into the carriage, which set off again.

The horse laboured up the hills, stumbled down them, and shambled horribly along the flat; at times he stopped dead.

'If we go on in this way,' I thought to myself, 'I shall not get to the Crossways till long after my hosts have finished dinner; and even'—here the horse stopped again—'after they have gone to bed.' I was very hungry and my temper was beginning to suffer. I tried to look at the landscape; without my having noticed it, the carriage had left the high-road and turned into a rough, narrow lane; the carriage lamps cast their light right and left on thick, high, uninterrupted hedges; they seemed to enclose us, to bar the road, to open out only just in time to let us through, and then the moment after to close up again behind us.

At the foot of a rather steeper hill the carriage stopped once more. The coachman came to the door, opened it, and said without further apology:

'Please to get down, mister. The hill is a bit steep for the horse.' He took the poor jade by the bridle and set off walking beside it. Half-way up the hill he turned round towards me as I was bringing up the rear:

'We shall soon be there now,' he said, in a milder tone. 'Look! there's the park!' And I saw in front of us a dark mass of trees blotting out part of the unclouded sky. It was an avenue of great beeches; we turned into it and struck the wider road we had recently left. The coachman invited me to get back into the carriage, and we soon reached the gate and turned into the garden.

It was too dark for me to make out the front of the château; the carriage set me down before a perron of three or four steps, which I went up, slightly dazed by a light that a woman who stood at the top was holding in her hand and casting down upon me. She was of no particular age, plain, thick-set, and shabbily dressed. She gave me rather a stiff nod. I bowed in some uncertainty....

'Madame Floche, no doubt? ...'

'No, only Mademoiselle Verdure. Monsieur and Madame Floche have gone to bed. They beg you to excuse them for not being here to receive you; but we dine early.'

'But you, Mademoiselle? I'm afraid I have kept you up late.'

'Oh, I'm accustomed to it,' she said without turning round. She had preceded me into the hall. 'Perhaps you would like to take something?'

'I must admit I have not dined.'

She showed me into a vast dining-room, where a respect-able supper was laid out.

'At this time of night the kitchen fire is out; and in the country one must put up with what one can get.'

'But it all looks excellent,' I said, sitting down to a plate of cold meat. She herself settled sideways on a chair near the door; and during the whole time I was eating she stayed there, her eyes lowered, her hands crossed on her knees, in the deliberately assumed attitude of an underling. Several times when there was a pause in our uphill conversation, I apologized for detaining her; but she gave me to under-stand that she was waiting to clear away after I had finished:

'And how would you find your room all by yourself?'

I was making as much haste as I could and taking double-sized mouthfuls, when the door into the hall opened and a grey-haired priest with a rude-featured but pleasant face came in. He came towards me with outstretched hand.

'I was not going to put off the pleasure of welcoming our guest till tomorrow. I did not come down sooner because I knew you were talking to Mademoiselle Olympe Verdure,' he said, turning towards her with what looked like a teasing smile, while she sat with pursed-up lips and a wooden expression on her countenance.

'But now that you have finished eating,' he went on, as I rose, 'we will leave Mademoiselle Olympe to put things tidy; she will think it more proper, I presume, to allow a man to conduct Monsieur Lacase to his room and will re-sign that function to me.'

He bowed ceremoniously to Mademoiselle Verdure, who returned him a perfunctory curtsy.

'Oh! I resign; I resign ... I always resign to you, Mon-sieur l'Abbé, as you know. ...' Then she suddenly turned back:

'You were going to make me forget to ask Monsieur Lacase what he takes for breakfast.'

'Whatever you like, Mademoiselle. . . . What is the usual thing here?'

'Oh, anything. Tea for the ladies, coffee for Monsieur Floche, a plate of soup for Monsieur l'Abbé and Quaker Oats for Monsieur Casimir.'

'And you, Mademoiselle, do you take nothing?'

'Oh, I? Just *café au lait*.'

'If you will allow me, I will join you in taking *café au lait*.'

'Oh ho! Be careful, Mademoiselle,' said the Abbé, taking me by the arm. 'It looks to me very much as if Monsieur Lacase were making love to you!'

She shrugged her shoulders, then bowed to me quickly, while the Abbé carried me off.

My room was on the first floor, almost at the end of a passage.

'Here,' said the Abbé, opening the door of a spacious room in which a large wood fire was burning. 'God bless my soul! They've given you a fire. I dare say you would as soon have done without it. . . . It's true the nights in this part of the world are damp, and the season of this year is unusually rainy.'

He went up to the hearth, stretching out his huge hands towards the blaze, while at the same time he turned aside his face, in the attitude of a man of virtue warding off temptation. He seemed more inclined to talk than to let me sleep.

'So,' he began, catching sight of my trunk and hand-bag, 'Gratien has brought up your luggage.'

'Is Gratien the coachman who drove me here?' I asked.

'And the gardener too; for his duties as coachman cannot be said to take up much of his time.'

'Yes, he told me the barouche did not go out very often.'

'It's an historical event when it goes out. Besides, Monsieur de Saint-Auréol gave up his stables long ago; on grand occasions like tonight they borrow the farmer's horse.'

'Monsieur de Saint-Auréol?' I repeated in surprise.

'Yes,' he said; 'I know that it is Monsieur Floche you have come to see, but La Quartfourche belongs to his brother-in-law. Tomorrow you will have the honour of being presented to Monsieur and Madame de Saint-Auréol.'

'And who is the Monsieur Casimir who takes Quaker Oats for breakfast – the only thing I know about him?'

'Their grandson and my pupil. By God's permission, I have had charge of his education for the last three years.' He said this with his eyes closed and an air of devout humility as if he were talking of a prince of the blood.

'Are not his parents here?' I asked.

'Travelling.' He screwed up his lips and went on at once: 'I know, Monsieur, what noble, pious work brings you here ...'

'Oh, don't exaggerate its piety,' I interrupted, laughing. 'I am only interested in it from an historical point of view.'

'No matter,' said he, wafting aside any unpleasantness with a wave of his hand; 'history has its rights too. You will find Monsieur Floche the kindest, the surest of guides.'

'So my master, Monsieur Desnos, assured me.'

'Ah! You are a pupil of Albert Desnos?' He screwed up his lips again.

'Did you ever attend his lectures?' I had the imprudence to inquire.

'No,' he answered roughly. 'I know enough about him to be on my guard. ... An intellectual adventurer! At your age one is easily led astray by anything out of the ordinary. ...' And as I did not answer, 'His theories,' he went on, 'began by having some influence over the young; but it is already on the wane, I hear.'

I was much more inclined to sleep than to argue. Seeing he could not extract an answer out of me, he went on:

'Monsieur Floche's guidance will be less dangerous.'

Then, in face of a yawn I did not attempt to disguise:

'It's getting late,' he said. 'Tomorrow, if you allow it, we shall find time to continue our conversation. After your journey you must be tired.'

'I confess, Monsieur l'Abbé, I am dropping with sleep.'

As soon as he had left me, I took the logs off the fire, opened the windows wide, and flung back the shutters. A great rush of dark, damp air blew down the flame of my candle and I put it out so as better to contemplate the night. My room gave on to the park, but it was not on the front side of the house like those in the long passage, from which the view was no doubt far more extensive; mine was interrupted immediately by a mass of trees; there was barely a little space of sky left above them, in which the moon's crescent appeared for a moment, only to be hidden again the next by clouds. There had been more rain; the branches were still showering tears. ...

'All this doesn't seem to promise a very gay time,' thought I, as I closed the window and shutters. My moment's contemplation had chilled me through and through – soul even more than body; I piled on the logs again, made up the fire, and was delighted to find a hot-water bottle in my bed, placed there, no doubt, by the kind attention of Mademoiselle Verdure.

A moment later it occurred to me I had forgotten to put my shoes outside the door. I got up and stepped for a second into the passage; Mademoiselle Verdure was going by at the other end of the house. Her room was above mine, as I gathered from the heavy footsteps which shortly after began to shake my ceiling. Then a profound silence followed, and as I sank to sleep, the house, like a great ship, weighed anchor and started on its passage through the night.

CHAPTER TWO

I WAS wakened quite early by sounds from the kitchen, one door of which was immediately under my window. I pushed open the shutters and saw with delight an almost perfectly clear sky; the garden was still wet and glittering from a recent shower, and a bluish haze coloured the air. I was just going to shut my window again, when a boy came running out of the vegetable garden towards the kitchen. It was difficult to guess his age, for his face looked three or four years older than the rest of his body, which was badly deformed; his twisted legs gave him the most peculiar lurching gait and he progressed obliquely, or rather by a series of springs, almost as if he had a difficulty in getting one foot safely past the other. Obviously this must be Casimir, the Abbé's pupil. An enormous Newfoundland dog kept him company, gambolling at his side and jumping up at him with boisterous affection. The child kept him off as best he could, but just as they reached the kitchen, the dog, with a sudden bound, knocked him completely over and sent him rolling in the mud. A stout kitchen wench darted out, exclaiming as she picked the child up:

'Well, I never! A nice mess you're in now! Lord! How does the boy manage it! An't you been told scores o' times to leave Terno in the stable? Come along in with you and get wiped. . . .'

She dragged him into the kitchen. Just then there was a knock at my door; a maid had brought me my hot water. A quarter of an hour later the breakfast bell rang.

As I entered the dining-room, 'Madame Floche,' said the

Abbé, coming forward to meet me, 'here, I think, is our kind visitor.'

Madame Floche had risen from her chair, but seemed no taller standing than sitting. I made her a low bow, which she returned with an abrupt little bob. Some time or other some terrible event must have descended upon her and driven her head down between her shoulders, where it had remained ever since – and a little crooked too. Monsieur Floche had come to her side to greet me. The little old couple were of exactly the same height, dressed after the same fashion, looked the same age, seemed to be of one flesh. ... For a few moments we stood exchanging vague compliments, all three talking at once. Then a majestic silence fell and Mademoiselle Verdure came in carrying the tea-pot.

'Mademoiselle Olympe,' said Madame Floche at last (she was incapable of moving her head and therefore turned to address one from the waist upwards), 'our friend, Mademoiselle Olympe, was very anxious to know if you had slept well, and whether your bed was quite to your liking.'

I protested that it would have been impossible to sleep better and that the hot-water bottle I had found in my bed had been the greatest of comforts.

Then Mademoiselle Verdure, having wished me good-morning, went out again.

'And the noise from the kitchen did not disturb you too much this morning?'

I renewed my protestations.

'Do not hesitate to complain, I beg of you, for it would be perfectly easy to get another room ready....'

Monsieur Floche, without saying anything himself, nodded his head sideways and confirmed every word of his wife's with a smile.

'Yes, indeed,' said I, 'I can see it must be a very large

house, but I assure you I could not be more comfortably lodged.'

'Monsieur and Madame Floche,' said the Abbé, 'take a pleasure in spoiling their guests.'

Mademoiselle Olympe now brought in a plate of toast, pushing before her the little cripple whose tumble I had so lately witnessed. The Abbé seized him by the arm:

'Now then, Casimir, come along! You're not a baby now; come and say how-d'ye-do to Monsieur Lacase like a man. Put out your hand. Look up!'

Then, turning to me as if some excuse were necessary: 'We're not much used to company yet.'

The child's shyness made me feel uncomfortable.

'Is he your grandson?' I asked Madame Floche, quite forgetting the Abbé's information of the previous evening.

'Our great-nephew,' she replied; 'you will shortly be seeing my brother-in-law and my sister, who are his grand-parents.'

'He was afraid to come in because he had got his clothes muddy, playing with Terno,' exclaimed Mademoiselle Ver-dure.

'It was a funny kind of game,' said I, turning sympathetically to Casimir. 'I was at the window when he knocked you over. Didn't he hurt you?'

'We must let Monsieur Lacase know,' explained the Abbé in his turn, 'that a good balance is not one of our strong points. ...'

I could see that for myself, good Heavens! without its being necessary for him to point it out. And I took an immediate dislike to this great strapping, wall-eyed Abbé.

The child had given me no answer, but his face turned crimson. I was sorry for what I had said and afraid he might think I had meant some allusion to his infirmity. The Abbé, having finished his soup, had risen and was walking up and down the room. When not speaking he had a way of tightly closing his mouth so that it looked like the pursed-up, toothless mouth of a very old man. He came to a standstill behind Casimir, who was just scraping out his bowl.

'Come along, come along, young man! Avenzoar awaits us!'

The boy got up and they went out together.

As soon as breakfast was over, Monsieur Floche beckoned to me.

'Come with me into the garden, my young friend, and tell me how it fares with the world of intellectual Paris.'

Monsieur Floche's eloquence rose with the lark. Without paying much attention to my answers, he asked after his friend Gaston Boissier and various other learned men whom I might have studied under and with whom he still corresponded from time to time. He questioned me on my tasks, my studies, etc. I naturally said nothing about my literary projects and all I showed him of myself was the Sorbonne scholar. He then embarked on the history of La Quartfourche, from which place he had not stirred for nearly fifteen years – on the history, that is, of the park and house; the history of the family who had occupied it formerly was reserved for a later recital, but he began to tell me how he had become the possessor of certain seventeenth-century manuscripts which he thought might prove useful for my thesis. ... His steps, as he walked, or rather trotted, beside me, were very short and hurried. I noticed he wore his trousers so low that the fork came halfway down his thigh; the stuff hung in folds over his instep in front, but at the back, kept up by Heaven knows what mysterious device, it barely reached the top of his shoes. By this time, bemused by the soft warmth of the air and a kind of vegetable torpor, I was lending him a somewhat inattentive ear. We had followed an avenue of great chestnuts whose branches met overhead, and came out almost at the other end of the park. There was a bench there, shaded from the sun by a bush of smoke-tree,* and Monsieur Floche invited me to sit down.

'Did Abbé Santal tell you,' he began abruptly, 'that my brother-in-law was a little ...?' He did not finish the sentence, but touched his forehead with his forefinger.

I was too much taken aback to be able to think of anything to answer. He continued:

'Yes, the Baron de Saint-Auréol, my brother-in-law. Perhaps the Abbé has not told you so any more than he has me ... but all the same I know he thinks it; and so do I.... And about me, didn't the Abbé tell you I was a little ...?'

'Oh, Monsieur Floche, how can you imagine ...?'

'But, my dear young man,' said he, tapping me confidentially on the hand, 'I should think it only natural. Why not? We have fallen into habits down here, by shutting ourselves up so far from the world, which may be a little – out of the way perhaps. Nothing in the shape of – what shall I call it? – diversion, reaches us here. Yes, indeed. It was very kind of you to come and see us' – and as I attempted a movement in protest – 'I repeat, very kind, and I shall write this evening to my good friend Desnos and tell him so again: but, if you had any notion of confiding in me the things you have most at heart, the questions that trouble you, the problems that interest you – well! I feel sure I should not understand what you were saying.'

What answer could I make? I scratched the gravel with the end of my stick.

'You see,' he continued, 'we have a little lost touch down here. No, no! There's no need to protest. The Baron is as deaf as a post, but he's so vain that all he cares for

*Rhus cotinus, a kind of sumach, sometimes called wig tree.

is not to appear so; he had rather pretend to hear than make people speak louder. As for me, with regard to the opinions of the day, I believe I am as deaf as he; and as far as that goes, I don't complain. I don't really much try to understand. My long intercourse with Massillon and Bossuet has led me to believe that the problems which exercised their great minds are quite as noble and important as those which engrossed me in my youth – problems which their minds, great as they were, would certainly not have been able to understand – any more than I am able to understand those that engross you today. Therefore, with your consent, my dear colleague to be, you shall talk to me by preference of your studies, as they happen to be mine too, and you will forgive me if I do not question you as to the musicians, the poets, or the orators you most admire, nor as to the form of government you consider best.'

He took out an ancient turnip watch fastened to a black ribbon and looked at the time:

'Let us go in now,' said he, getting up. 'I feel my day is lost if I am not at work by ten o'clock.'

I offered him my arm, which he took, and if at moments I happened to slacken my pace on his account:

'Hasten! Hasten!' he would bid me. 'Thoughts are like flowers; those gathered in the morning keep fresh the longest.'

The library at La Quartfourche consists of two rooms separated only by a curtain. One, exceedingly small and raised by three steps above the other, is where Monsieur Floche works, at a table in front of the window. There is no view – nothing but the branches of elm or alder brushing against the panes; on the table stands an old-fashioned oil lamp with a green porcelain shade to it; under the table a huge foot-muff; in one corner a little stove; in the other a second table piled with lexicons; between the two a cupboard fitted as a filing cabinet. The second room is immense, its walls are lined to the ceiling with books; it has two windows; a big table stands in the centre.

'This is where you are to sit,' said Monsieur Floche; and as I uttered an exclamation, 'No, no! I am used to my little den,' he said; 'to tell the truth, it suits me best; I feel I can concentrate better here. Do not scruple to use the big table, and, if you like, we can draw the curtain so as not to disturb each other.'

'Not on my account,' I protested; 'if I had had to be alone all this time in order to work, I should never . . .'

'Very well,' he replied without letting me finish, 'then we will leave it undrawn. For my part it will be a great pleasure to me to be able to catch a glimpse of you now and then out of the corner of my eye.'

(And, as a fact, in the days that followed I never lifted my head from my work without meeting the old fellow's eye. He would smile and nod at me, or hurriedly look the other way for fear of disturbing me, and pretend to be deep in his papers.)

He set to work at once, arranging the books and manuscripts likely to interest me, so that I could most easily get at them. They were kept for the most part in the filing cabinet in the little room; their number and importance greatly surpassed the account Monsieur Desnos had given of them; it would take me a week at least, I could see, to extract all the treasures of information they contained. Finally, Monsieur Floche opened a very small cupboard next the cabinet and took out of it the famous 'Bossuet Bible', in which, opposite the verses he had used as texts, the Eagle of Meaux had inscribed the dates of the sermons they had inspired. I expressed astonishment that Albert

Desnos had made no use of these entries in his writings; but the book had only recently come into Monsieur Floche's hands.

'As a matter of fact, I did write a memoir on the subject,' he continued, 'and am glad now not to have communicated it to anyone yet, as it may prove useful to you for your thesis and will be entirely new.'

Again I expostulated:

'Whatever merits my thesis may have, I shall owe it to your kindness. I hope at least I may be allowed to dedicate it to you, Monsieur Floche, as a very small mark of my gratitude.'

He smiled a little sadly:

'When one is so near leaving this world, one gives a welcome to anything that promises any kind of survival.'

I felt it would have been unsuitable for me to improve upon this.

'And now,' he went on, 'you will take possession of the library and only remember my presence if there is anything you want to ask me. Take the papers you want with you.... Au revoir! ...' And as I went down the three steps and turned my head to smile at him, he waved his hand in return: 'Au revoir!'

I carried off with me into the big room the necessary papers with which to start my work. Without leaving the table at which I sat I could still see Monsieur Floche in his little 'den'. He fidgeted about for a few minutes, opening and shutting drawers, pulling out papers and putting them back, with all the appearance of being a very busy man. ... I could not help suspecting that he was a good deal disturbed, not to say put out, by my presence and that in his usually well-ordered existence the slightest shock was likely to endanger his mental equilibrium. At last he settled down, plunged knee-deep into the foot-muff and remained motion-less. . . .

I also made a pretence of being absorbed in my work, but I found it very difficult to control my thoughts; I did not even attempt to. Those thoughts of mine went circling round La Quartfourche as if it were a fortress the entrance to which I had perforce to find. Was I subtle? – That was what I wished to be sure of. 'Now, my friend,' said I to myself, 'you would-be writer of novels, we shall see what you are made of! Description? Heaven forbid! That is not what is wanted here – but to discover the reality beneath the semblance. . . . In the short space of time allowed you for your stay at La Quartfourche, if you let one gesture escape you – one twitch even – without immediately ac-counting for it to yourself, psychologically, historically, and completely, it will be because you don't know your job.'

And I once more turned to look at Monsieur Floche; he sat with his profile towards me and I saw a big, flabby, inexpressive nose, bushy eyebrows, a clean-shaven chin, con-tinually on the move as though chewing a quid . . . and I thought to myself that nothing can make a face more im-penetrable than the mask of kindliness.

The luncheon bell surprised me in the midst of these reflections.

CHAPTER THREE

IT was at that same lunch that Monsieur Floche, without a word of oratorical warning, led me into the presence of the Saint-Auréol couple. The Abbé at least might have dropped me a hint the night before. I remember having experienced the same feeling of stupefaction once upon a time at the Zoological Gardens, when I first made the acquaintance of the *Phoenicopterus antiquorum*, or the spatula-beaked flamingo.* It is impossible to say whether the Baron or the Baronne was the more peculiar; they made a perfect pair – like the Floches for that matter; in a museum they would have been placed in the same glass case without a moment's hesitation and labelled 'extinct species'. When I first saw them, I experienced the same kind of ill-defined admiration that fills one on first seeing a perfectly accomplished work of art, or one of the wonders of nature – things that leave one stupid with amazement and incapable of any analysis of one's feelings. It was only gradually that I managed to unravel my impressions. . . .

Baron Narcisse de Saint-Auréol wore knee-breeches, shoes with very striking buckles, a cravat and jabot of muslin. There emerged from the opening of his collar an Adam's apple which was quite as prominent as his chin, though it did its best to escape notice amidst the billowing muslin; at the slightest movement of his jaw, his chin made a desperate effort to meet his nose, to which that feature gallantly responded. One of his eyes remained hermetically closed; the corner of his mouth and all the lines of his face were

* Gérard is mistaken – the beak of the *Phoenicopterus antiquorum* is not spatula-shaped. (Author's note.)

screwed up towards the other, which shone brightly from behind a sheltering cheekbone and seemed to exclaim: 'Beware! I am here alone, but nothing escapes me!'

Madame de Saint-Auréol was almost entirely hidden in floods of false lace. Her long hands, loaded with enormous rings, lay idle and trembling in the depths of her fluttering sleeves. A kind of hood made of black taffeta, lined with tatters of white lace, shrouded her face; it was tied under her chin with two taffeta strings, which were white with the powder that fell from her terrifically painted face. When I came in, she struck an attitude in front of me, standing sideways with her head thrown back, and exclaimed in a high, loud, uninflected voice:

'There was a time, Sister, when more respect was shown to the name of Saint-Auréol . . .'

Whom was she attacking? No doubt she wanted to make me feel, and to make her sister feel, that I was not the guest of the Floches; for she continued, bending her head affectedly to one side, and raising her right hand towards me:

'The Baron and I have much pleasure, Monsieur, in receiving you at our table.'

I applied my lips to one of her rings and raised my head from the ceremony blushing, for my position between the Saint-Auréols and the Floches threatened to be embarrassing. But Madame Floche appeared to pay no attention to her sister's outburst. As for the Baron, his existence seemed to me problematical, although he was all honey and amiability as far as I was concerned. During the whole of my stay at La Quartfourche he could not be persuaded to call me anything but Monsieur de La Case; which gave him the opportunity of declaring he had met several of my relations at the Tuileries . . . one of my uncles in particular, who used to play piquet with him.

'Ah! he was a queer fellow! Every time he played a trump, he used to shout out: "Domino!"...'

The Baron's conversation was almost entirely of this calibre. At table he was almost the only person to speak; and then, as soon as the meal was over, he sank into a mummy-like silence.

As we were leaving the dining-room, Madame Floche came up to me and said in a whisper:

'Perhaps you would be so kind, Monsieur Lacase, as to favour me with a few minutes' talk?' A talk which apparently she did not wish anyone to hear, for she began by leading me off in the direction of the kitchen-garden, saying out loud that she wanted to show me the espaliers.

'It is about my great-nephew,' she began, as soon as she was sure we were out of hearing. .... 'I should not like you to think I am criticizing Abbé Santal's teaching ... but I thought that you, who live in such close proximity to the very fountain-head of learning' (those were her words), 'might give us some advice.'

'You have only to speak, Madame Floche. I will do whatever I can.'

'Well then, for so young a child, I am afraid the subject of his thesis is a little out of the way.'

'What thesis?' I asked, feeling slightly at a loss.

'The thesis for his *baccalauréat*.'*

'Oh, of course,' I answered, resolving for the future to be astonished at nothing. 'On what subject?'

'Well, Monsieur l'Abbé is afraid that a literary or purely philosophical subject may be too conducive to vagueness in a young mind already over-inclined to day-dreaming ... (that, at least, is what the Abbé says). He has therefore urged Casimir to choose an historical subject.'

*An elementary examination for which no thesis is required.

98

'A point of view for which there is a great deal to be said. And what is the subject?'

'You must excuse me. I am afraid of mis-pronouncing the name ... Averrhoes.'

'The Abbé no doubt had reasons for choosing the subject, which at first sight might seem, it is true, a little peculiar.'

'They chose it together. As for the reasons the Abbé put forward, I am quite prepared to endorse them. The anecdotic interest of the subject, he says, is particularly likely to fix Casimir's attention, which is a little given to wandering. And then it has never been treated before, and apparently that is a thing to which the examiners attach the greatest importance.'

'I cannot remember, it is true ...'

'And naturally, in order to find a subject that has never been treated before, one has to leave the beaten road.'

'Of course!'

'Only, I will tell you what troubles me. ... But perhaps I am trespassing on your time?'

'Please believe I am most anxious to be of help to you.'

'Well then, it is this. I make no doubt that Casimir will soon be able to pass his thesis fairly brilliantly, but I am afraid that this desire to specialize this slightly premature desire – may lead the Abbé to neglect his general education a little – sums, for instance, or astronomy.'

'And what does Monsieur Floche think about it?' I asked in bewilderment.

'Oh! Monsieur Floche approves of everything the Abbé says or does.'

'And the parents?'

'They have put us in charge of the child,' said she after a slight hesitation: then, stopping short in her walk:

'As a mark of your kindness, dear Monsieur Lacase,' said she, 'I should be very glad if you would talk to Casimir

99

a little – without seeming actually to question him – and especially not before the Abbé, as he might perhaps take offence. I feel sure that in that way . . .'

'With the greatest pleasure in the world, I assure you. I shall certainly have no difficulty in finding some excuse for going out with your nephew. He can show me part of the park.'

'He is a little shy at first with people he doesn't know, but he has a confiding nature.'

'I have no doubt we shall soon be very good friends.'

A little later, when we were assembled again for tea:

'Casimir,' said Madame Floche, 'you should show Monsieur Lacase the quarry; I am sure it will interest him.' Then, coming up to me:

'Go quick, before the Abbé comes down, or he will offer to go with you.'

I went out into the park at once, while the child, hobbling beside me, pointed out the way.

'I suppose it's recreation time,' I began.

He did not answer. I went on:

'Do you never work after tea?'

'Oh, yes; but I have done my copying for the day.'

'What is it you copy?'

'The thesis.'

'Ah . . .'

After a little beating about the bush, I succeeded in finding out that this thesis was a work of the Abbé's, which he made the boy, who wrote a good hand, copy out for him. He was making four fair copies in four cloth-bound copybooks, of which he covered a certain number of pages every day. Casimir declared for that matter he liked 'copying' very much.

'But why four times?'

'Because I don't remember properly.'

'Do you understand what you write?'

'Sometimes. Other times the Abbé explains it to me, or else he says I shall understand it when I'm older.'

The Abbé had simply turned his pupil into a kind of copying-machine. Was that how he understood his duties? I felt my heart swell with indignation and determined to have a dramatic conversation with him as soon as possible. In my anger I had unconsciously hurried my pace and Casimir kept up with me with some difficulty; I noticed he was dripping with perspiration. I gave him my hand, which he held in his as he limped along beside me, and at the same time I slackened my pace.

'Is the thesis your only work?'

'Oh, no,' said he at once; but when I questioned him further, it soon became apparent that he did very little else. He no doubt felt my astonishment.

'I read a great deal,' he added, in the kind of voice in which a person in poor circumstances might say: 'I have some other clothes.'

'And what do you like reading?'

'Travels.' Then, looking at me with eyes in which confidence had taken the place of inquiry: 'The Abbé has been to China. Did you know?' And his voice expressed boundless admiration – veneration – for his master.

We had now reached the part of the park Madame Floche called the quarry. Long since abandoned, this quarry formed a kind of grotto in the side of the hill, the entrance to which was hidden by bushes. We sat down on a boulder of rock in the warmth of the setting sun. There was no enclosure at this end of the park; on our left hand, a path ran slanting downhill and was fenced off at the bottom by a small railing. Everywhere else the slope of the ground was steep enough to serve as a natural protection.

'And you, Casimir, have you ever travelled?' I asked.

He made no answer, and sat with his head down. ...
The little valley at our feet was filling with shade; in front
of us the landscape was shut out by a hill which the rays
of the sun had already begun to touch and which was
crowned by a clump of oaks and Spanish chestnuts that
grew on a chalky mound riddled with the holes of a rabbit-
warren. The rather romantic aspect of the place was set
off by the uniform softness of the surrounding country.

'Look at the rabbits!' cried Casimir suddenly; then, after
a moment he pointed to the clump of trees and added:
'I went up there one day with Monsieur l'Abbé.'

On our way home we passed by a pond overgrown with
weeds. I promised Casimir to prepare him a line and show
him how to fish for frogs.

This first evening of mine, which was brought to a close
very little after nine o'clock, differed in no particular
from those that followed it, and, I suppose, from those that
had preceded it, for my hosts had the good taste not to
treat me with any special ceremony. Immediately after
dinner we repaired to the drawing-room, where Gratien in
the meantime had lighted the fire. A large lamp, placed at
one end of a marquetry table, lighted a game of backgammon which the Baron and the Abbé started at the further
end of the table, and a small card-table as well, where the
ladies sat down to a lively kind of Oriental bezique.

'Monsieur Lacase, who is accustomed to the dissipations
of Paris, will no doubt consider our game a little dull. ...'
Madame de Saint-Auréol had begun by saying.

In the meantime, Monsieur Floche dozed in an arm-chair
by the fire; Casimir sat ploughing his way through a book
of Pictures of the World, his elbows on the table, his head
in his hands, his mouth open and slobbering. Partly to
appear at ease and partly from politeness, I pretended to
take a violent interest in the ladies' bezique; it could be

played like whist with a dummy, but four made a better
game, so that when I offered to take a hand, Madame de
Saint-Auréol accepted me as a partner with enthusiasm.
The first evening or two, my blunders brought our side to
disaster, and were the delight of Madame Floche, who, after
every triumph, took the liberty of giving my arm a discreet
little tap with her mittened hand. There were all sorts of
openings for boldness, cunning and finesse. Mademoiselle
Olympe played a cautious, deliberate game. At the beginning of each hand, the players made their stakes, and
ventured to double or not according to the cards they held,
which gave a little room for bluff; Madame de Saint-Auréol
used to launch out recklessly, her eyes shining, her cheeks
scarlet and her chin in a tremble; when she had a really
good hand, she would fetch me a great kick under the
table; Mademoiselle Olympe did what she could to stand
up to her, but she was completely demoralized by the old
lady, who, instead of calling another number, would suddenly burst out in a shrill voice with:

'Verdure, that's a lie!'

At the end of the first game, Madame Floche would take
out her watch and, as if it were really the exact hour:

'Casimir!' she would call out, 'come, Casimir, it's bed-
time.'

The boy seemed to wake painfully out of his lethargy,
rose, offered the gentlemen his limp hand, the ladies his
cheek, and then left the room, dragging his foot behind
him.

As Madame de Saint-Auréol invited us to our revenge,
the first game of backgammon would come to an end; then
Monsieur Floche would sometimes take his brother-in-law's
place; neither Monsieur Floche nor the Abbé called their
throws, so that nothing was heard from their end but the
rattling of the dice in the box and on to the table; Monsieur

de Saint-Auréol soliloquized or hummed a tune in the arm-chair, and sometimes he would smash violently at the fire with the tongs, and so recklessly that the red-hot-cinders were scattered far and wide; upon which Mademoiselle Olympe would hastily dash to the rescue and perform what Madame de Saint-Auréol elegantly termed 'the spark-dance' on the carpet. . . . Oftener than not, Monsieur Floche left the Abbé to wrestle with the Baron and remained in his arm-chair; I could see him from my place, not sleeping as he said, but shaking his head in the shadow; and the first evening, when a spurt of flame suddenly lighted his face, I saw that he was crying.

By a quarter past nine the game of bezique was over, and Madame Floche put out the lamp, while Mademoiselle Verdure lighted two candelabras, which she placed on each side of the backgammon-board.

'Don't keep him up too long, Abbé,' exhorted Madame de Saint-Auréol, giving her husband's shoulder a tap with her fan.

On the first night – and indeed on all the subsequent ones – I thought it the proper thing to obey the ladies' signal and leave the backgammon players to their game and Monsieur Floche, who was the last to go upstairs, to his meditations. In the hall, everyone took possession of a candle and the ladies wished me good-night to the same accompaniment of curtsies as in the morning. I went to my room. Soon after I heard the gentlemen come up. And soon after that all was quiet. But for a long time light was to be seen filtering under some of the doors. And an hour or more later, if for any reason one had to go into the passage, one ran the risk of coming upon Madame Floche or Mademoiselle Verdure in night attire, attending to some last household duty. Later still, and when one would have thought every light must be extinguished, a shadow could be seen on the pane of a little closet, which had a window opening on to the passage, but no door – the shadow of Madame de Saint-Auréol sitting over her mending.

CHAPTER FOUR

My second day at La Quartfourche very appreciably resembled the first – even from hour to hour; but any curiosity I may have had concerning the doings of my hosts had now entirely subsided. Ever since morning the rain had been coming down in a steady drizzle. As it was impossible to go out and the ladies' conversation was becoming more and more trifling, I spent practically the whole day over my work. It was all I could do to get a few words with the Abbé after lunch; he invited me to smoke a cigarette with him in a kind of glass house just off the drawing-room, which was called, rather pompously, 'the orangery', and was the place in which the few seats and chairs used in the garden were stored during the wet weather.

'But, my dear Sir,' he said, when I tackled him a little nervously on the subject of the boy's education, 'I should have been only too glad to give Casimir the benefit of my feeble resources; it was with no small regret that I gave up the attempt. With that limp of his would you have suggested my teaching him to dance on the tight-rope? I very soon found I had to come down in my aims. If he is studying Averrhoes with me now, it is because I am engaged in writing a treatise on the philosophy of Aristotle, and rather than keep droning on with the child over the rudiments of spelling or what not, I took a heartfelt pleasure in associating him with my own work. It is as good a subject as any other. The important thing is to keep Casimir busy for three or four hours during the day. Surely some feeling of irritation would have been unavoidable if I had to waste an equal amount of my own time? And with no profit to him, I

assure you. Enough on this subject now, don't you think?'
Upon which, throwing away his unfinished cigarette, he
got up and returned to the drawing-room.

The bad weather prevented me from going out with
Casimir, and we had to put off the proposed fishing expedition till next day; but to make up for the child's disappointment I racked my brains to find some other amusement for him. Finally I managed to get hold of a chess-
board and taught him to play 'fox and geese', which game
engrossed him till supper-time.

The evening began in exactly the same way as the day
before, but I had already given up looking at or listening
to anybody; a feeling of unspeakable boredom had begun to
weigh me down.

Directly after dinner, a kind of squall came up. Twice
over, Mademoiselle Verdure interrupted the bezique to see
whether the rain was 'driving' into the upstairs rooms.
We had to play the return match without her; there was
no spirit in it whatever. By the fire, in a low chair, generally
spoken of as the *berline*, Monsieur Floche, lulled by the
sound of the downpour, had actually fallen asleep, while
the Baron, sitting opposite him in the *bergère*, groaned
and grunted over his rheumatism.

'A game of backgammon would take your thoughts off,'
the Abbé kept repeating in vain; finally, however, seeing
there was no hope of an adversary, he went off to bed,
taking Casimir with him.

When, that evening, I found myself once more alone in
my room, I was assailed, body and soul, by a feeling of
intolerable wretchedness – an ennui so great that it almost
took the shape of fear. Here I was, separated from all the
rest of the world by a wall of rain, remote from all passion,
remote from life, imprisoned in a dreary nightmare among
a set of strange beings, scarcely to be called human –

cold-blooded, colourless creatures whose hearts had long since ceased to beat. I opened my portmanteau and snatched up my railway guide. A train! No matter the time, day or night – oh, for a train to carry me away! This is stifling me. . . .

Impatience prevented me from sleeping for a long while.

When I awoke the next morning, though my determination was perhaps no less fixed, yet I felt it impossible to be so lacking in courtesy to my hosts as to go off without inventing some excuse for curtailing my visit so suddenly. I had actually been rash enough to talk of staying at least a week at La Quartfourche! Well, what of it? I must receive some bad news summoning me back to Paris. . . . Fortunately, I had left my address behind me, with directions for my letters to be forwarded to La Quartfourche; it would really be a miracle, I thought, if I did not get some kind of envelope that very day which, with a little skill, would serve my turn . . . and all my hope was fixed on the arrival of the postman. He generally appeared shortly after twelve, while we were finishing lunch; before we left the table, Delphine would bring in the meagre little packet of letters and papers which she took to Madame Floche, who then distributed them to the rest of the party. It happened that day unfortunately that the Abbé Santal had been invited to lunch by the priest of Pont-l'Évêque, and at about eleven he had come to take leave of Monsieur Floche and me. It did not strike me at the time that he was doing me out of the horse and trap.

So that at lunch I went through the little performance I had prepared beforehand.

'Dear, dear! How tiresome!' I murmured as I opened one of the envelopes handed me by Madame Floche; and as my hosts very tactfully refrained from noticing this exclamation, I began again rather more emphatically: 'What a bit of bad luck!' acting surprise and dismay, as I gazed at a perfectly inoffensive note. At last Madame Floche ventured to ask timidly:

'No bad news, I hope?'

'Oh, nothing really serious,' I replied at once, 'but what puts me out is that I fear I shall have to return to Paris immediately.'

The consternation from one end of the table to the other was general and so much greater than I had expected that I felt myself blushing in confusion. It showed itself to begin with in a melancholy silence; then at last Monsieur Floche said in rather a shaky voice:

'Do you really mean it, my dear young friend? But your work! But our ...'

He was unable to finish. I could think of nothing to say, nothing to answer, and upon my word, was not a little upset myself. My eyes were fixed on the top of Casimir's head, who with his nose in his plate went on chopping an apple into little bits. Mademoiselle Verdure had turned scarlet with indignation.

'I hardly like to press you to stay,' hazarded Madame Floche feebly.

'For any inducement La Quartfourche may have to offer!' Madame de Saint-Auréol added acidly.

'Oh, dear lady, I beg you to believe, nothing ...' I was beginning to expostulate, but without attending to me, she shouted into the ear of her husband, who was sitting next her:

'Monsieur Lacase wants to leave us!'

'Delightful! Delightful! Most kind ...' said the deaf man, smiling at me.

In the meantime, Madame Floche was consulting Mademoiselle Verdure.

'But how shall we manage – and the mare just gone with the Abbé?'

I here conceded a trifle:

'As long as I get to Paris the first thing tomorrow morning ... I could make the evening train do.'

'Let Gratien go at once to see if we can have Bouligny's horse. Say it will be wanted to catch the ...' then, turning to me, 'will the seven o'clock do?'

'Oh, Madame Floche, I am truly sorry to be giving you so much trouble.'

Lunch came to an end in silence. Immediately afterwards, little Monsieur Floche carried me off, and as soon as we were alone in the passage leading to the library, the old fellow began:

'But, my dear Sir – my dear boy – I can't yet believe ... but you still have to go through a pile of ... Is it really possible? What a piece of ill-luck! What a very sad piece of ill-luck! And I was just waiting till you had finished this first bit of work before handing you over some other papers I had got out last night. I was counting on them, I must confess, to give you a fresh interest and keep you with us a little longer. Well, I shall have to let you see them at once. Come along. We still have some time before evening – for I suppose I mustn't ask you to come back again?'

The old man's concern made me feel ashamed of myself. I had been hard at it all the previous day and the whole of the morning, so that in reality there was not much left for me to glean from the first set of papers confided to me by Monsieur Floche; but as soon as we had got up into his retreat he proceeded to pull open a drawer, from the recesses of which he mysteriously extracted a packet wrapped in linen and tied up with a bit of string into which was slipped a docket, bearing the descriptions and sources of the papers to serve as index.

'Take the whole packet,' he said; 'I dare say it's not all

of it worth much, but you will be able to sort out whatever is likely to interest you, quicker than I should.'

While he was busy again, opening and shutting one drawer after another, I went down into the library and spread the bundle out on the big table.

Some of the papers certainly did bear on the subject of my work, but there were not many of them and they were of very little importance. The greater number, in Monsieur Floche's own handwriting, dealt with the life of Massillon and were consequently of no use to me.

Could this really have been what poor old Floche had relied on to keep me at La Quartfourche? I looked at him. He had now sunk back into his foot-muff and was engaged with a pin in carefully cleaning out the holes of a little kind of pepperbox, which he used for sprinkling sandarac* on his paper. This operation over, he raised his head and met my eyes. Such a friendly smile illuminated his countenance that I got up to have a chat with him.

'Monsieur Floche,' said I, as I leant on the lintel at the entrance to his little sanctum, 'why do you never come to Paris? We should all be so delighted to see you there.'

'At my age moving is difficult and expensive.'

'And you don't miss town too much?'

'Bah!' he said, throwing up his hands, 'I was prepared to miss it more than I did. Just at first, the solitude of the country does seem rather hard to anyone who loves talking; but one gets accustomed to it.'

'Then it was not from inclination that you came to live at La Quartfourche?'

He disentangled himself from his foot-muff, stood up,

*A kind of resinous gum, which, when reduced to powder, was used by Monsieur Floche and his contemporaries to sprinkle over writing-paper, in order to prevent it from becoming spongy after words had been erased by a pen-knife.

and putting his hand familiarly on my sleeve, he said:

'I had a few colleagues at the Institute for whom I felt some affection, and among them your dear master Albert Desnos; I really think I was in a fair way to take my place among them . . .'

It seemed as if he wished to add something, but I did not venture to put a too direct question:

'Was it Madame Floche who was so much attracted by the country?'

'N–o. Still it was on Madame Floche's account I came; but she herself was summoned here by a little family occurrence.'

He had come down into the large room and caught sight of the packet which I had already tied up again.

'Ah, you have been through it already,' he said sadly. 'And doubtless there was not much you could make use of. Well! well! There it is! I pick up the very smallest crumbs, I know; sometimes I tell myself I am wasting my time gathering straws. But people like myself are needed for these trifling labours, so as to spare others like you who will be able to turn them to brilliant account. It will give me the greatest pleasure, as I read your thesis, to feel that the pains I took may have been of just a little use to you.'

Just then the bell summoned us to tea.

How was I to discover, thought I, what this 'little family occurrence' could be which had been important enough to make these two old people take such a decision? Did the Abbé know it? Instead of setting myself against him, I should have tried to get round him. It couldn't be helped! It was too late now. All the same, Monsieur Floche was a worthy man whom I should always remember kindly.

'Casimir doesn't dare to ask,' said Madame Floche, as we entered the dining-room, 'whether you would take another little turn with him in the garden. It's what he would very much like, I know, but perhaps you haven't time.'

The child was choking over his cup of milk. 'I was just going to suggest it,' I answered; 'I have managed to get even with my work and I shall be free now till it's time to start. It seems to have stopped raining too, I see.' . . . And I took him off with me into the park.

At the first turn in the path, the child, who was holding one of my hands in both his, pressed it against his burning cheek and kept it there.

'You said you were going to stay a week,' he said.

'My dear little fellow, I can't stay any longer.'

'You're bored.'

'No! But I have to go.'

'Where are you going?'

'To Paris. But I shall come back again.' He looked anxiously at me, as I said the words.

'Really and truly? Do you promise?'

The child's question was so trustful I had not the heart to retract.

'Would you like me to write it on a bit of paper for you to keep?'

'Oh yes!' he exclaimed, kissing my hand with fervour and taking frantic leaps to show his delight.

'And now, do you know what I think would be very nice? Instead of going to fish, suppose we were to pick some flowers for your aunt? Then you and I could take a big bouquet into her room as a surprise for her.'

I had vowed to myself not to leave La Quartfourche without having been into the room of one or other of the two old ladies; as they were continually going up and downstairs all over the house, I ran a great risk of being disturbed in my indiscreet investigations; I relied now on the boy as an excuse for my presence. However strange it might appear for me to follow him into his grandmother's or aunt's room, the bouquet would be a good enough pretext to keep me in countenance, in case of a surprise.

But picking flowers at La Quartfourche was not such an easy matter as I had supposed. Gratien kept a most suspicious eye on the whole garden. He not only pointed out what flowers it was permissible to pick, but was jealously particular as to the way in which they were picked. One had to take pruning-scissors or knife – and such precautions! This was all explained to me by Casimir. Gratien accompanied us to a bed of magnificent dahlias from which bouquets without number might have been taken and never missed.

'Above the bud, Master Casimir; how many times must you be told? Always cut above the bud.'

'At the end of the season like this, it's not of the slightest importance,' I cried impatiently.

'It's always important,' he growled in reply; 'and there's never a season for doing wrong.'

I cannot stand these sententious grumblers. . . .

The child went ahead of me carrying the flowers. As we passed through the hall, I possessed myself of a vase. . . .

A deep religious peace filled the room; the shutters were closed; near the bed, in the depths of an alcove and at the foot of a little crucifix of ivory and ebony, stood a mahogany prie-dieu covered with dark red velvet. Across the crucifix, and half concealing it, lay a small sprig of box, hanging from a pink ribbon and fastened to one arm of the cross. The quiet solemnity of the hour came like a call to prayer. Forgetting what I had come for and the vain curiosity that had brought me to the spot, I left Casimir to arrange the flowers according to his fancy on the corner of a chest of drawers, and looked at nothing more in the room: 'It is here then,' I thought, 'in this great bed, that good old

Madame Floche will soon be ending her quiet days, sheltered from every breath of life. ... O ships questing for storms, how tranquil a haven is this!'

In the meantime, Casimir was getting impatient with his flowers; the heavy-headed dahlias had been too much for him and the whole bouquet had toppled over on to the floor.

'Do come and help me,' said he at last.

But when I took his place and began struggling with the flowers, he ran across to a bureau at the other end of the room and proceeded to open it.

'I'm going to write the promise for you to sign about coming back,' he said.

'That's right,' I replied, still keeping up my little piece of humbug. 'Be quick though; your aunt might be cross if she saw you fumbling about in her writing-table.'

'Oh, my aunt's in the kitchen; besides, she never scolds me.'

In the most painstaking fashion he covered a piece of notepaper with his handwriting.

'Now come and sign.'

I went over to the writing-table.

'But, Casimir,' I said laughing, 'there's no need for *you* to sign too!' The child, no doubt in order to make the engagement more binding and to give himself the impression that he too was pledging his word, had thought proper to put his own name at the bottom of the page, on which he had written:

Monsieur Lacase promises to come back to La Quartfourche next year.

Casimir de Saint-Auréol

My laughter and comment disconcerted him for a moment; he himself had taken the whole thing so seriously to heart! Was it possible that I was not in earnest? He was on the verge of tears.

'Make room then,' I said, 'and let me sign.'

He got up and, when I had signed the paper, jumped for joy and covered my hand with kisses. Then, just as I was on the point of leaving, he caught hold of my sleeve and bent over the writing-table once more.

'I'll show you something,' he said, pressing a spring and sliding out a drawer of which he knew the secret; then, after groping about a little among old bills and scraps of ribbon, he held out to me a delicately framed miniature:

'Look!'

I took it with me to the window.

In what fairy story is it that the prince falls in love with the princess's portrait without having seen her?

This must have been the very portrait. I know nothing about painting and take very little interest in its technical qualities; no doubt a connoisseur would have pronounced the miniature affected: character had been almost obliterated by a too flattering insistence on grace; but the grace was there, and so pure and perfect as to be unforgettable.

I cared very little, as I have said, about the good or bad points of the painting: the young woman I had before me showed her profile only; one temple half hidden by a heavy dark curl; a languid eye, dreamy and melancholy; half opened lips, as if just parted in a sigh, and a slender neck, fragile as the stem of a flower. It was a face of the most disturbing, the most angelic beauty. I lost all consciousness of hour and place as I gazed at it. Casimir, who had left me to put the finishing touches to the flowers, came back and bent over the portrait:

'That's my Mamma. Isn't she pretty?'

I felt almost ashamed in the child's presence to think his mother so beautiful.

'Where is your Mamma now?'

'I don't know.'

'Why isn't she here?'

'She's bored here.'

'And your father?'

He hung his head, a little confused and shame-faced, and answered:

'My father is dead.'

My questions made him uncomfortable, but I was determined to go on.

'I suppose your Mamma comes to see you sometimes?'

'Oh, yes, often!' he replied with conviction and raised his head quickly. Then he added in a lower voice:

'She comes to talk to my aunt.'

'But doesn't she talk to you too?'

'Oh, I can't talk to her ... and besides I'm in bed when she comes.'

'In bed!'

'Yes, she comes at night. ...' Then his trustfulness got the better of him (I had put down the portrait and he had taken hold of my hand) and he added tenderly, and almost as if it were a secret he was telling me:

'Last time she came and kissed me in bed.'

'Then doesn't she generally kiss you?'

'Oh yes, often.'

'Then why do you say "last time"?'

'Because she was crying.'

'Was she with your aunt?'

'No, she came in all by herself, in the dark. She thought I was asleep.'

'Did she wake you up?'

'Oh, I wasn't asleep. I was waiting till she came.'

'You knew she was there then?'

He looked down again without answering. I insisted:

'How did you know she was there?'

No answer. I still went on:

'How could you see she was crying in the dark?'

'Oh, I could feel it.'

'Didn't you ask her to stay?'

'Oh, yes, I did. She was bending over my bed; I took hold of her hair ...'

'And what did she say?'

'She laughed. She said I was making her hair untidy – but that she had to go.'

'Then she doesn't love you?'

'Oh yes, she loves me very much,' he cried, so passionately and with such a scarlet face, as he drew abruptly back from my side, that I felt ashamed of my question.

Madame Floche's voice was suddenly heard calling from the foot of the stairs:

'Casimir! Casimir! Go and tell Monsieur Lacase that it's time for him to get ready. The carriage will be here in half an hour.'

I sprang up and dashed downstairs to where the old lady was standing in the hall.

'Madame Floche!' I cried, 'is there anyone who could take a telegram for me? I have thought of a plan. I believe I can arrange to stay a few more days with you.'

She took me by both hands:

'Oh, dear Monsieur Lacase, how very unlikely! ...' And as, in her emotion, she could think of nothing else to say, she kept on repeating: 'How very unlikely!' ... At last, running out, she called up to Monsieur Floche's window: 'Good man! Good man!' (that was her name for him) 'Monsieur Lacase has consented to stay.'

Her feeble voice, shrill and cracked though it was, succeeded in reaching him; I saw the window open. Monsieur

Floche looked out for a moment, and as soon as he understood the situation, called to me:

'I'll come down! I'll come down!'

Casimir joined him, and for several minutes I had to
confront their joint congratulations; I might have been
one of the family.

I wrote some kind of fantastic message by way of telegram and had it dispatched to an imaginary address.

'I'm afraid,' said Madame Floche, 'I was a little indiscreet
at lunch and pressed you too much to stay. I hope, if you
do, your affairs in Paris won't suffer?'

'I hope not, dear lady; I have asked a friend to see to
them for me.'

Madame de Saint-Auréol now appeared on the scene.
She walked round the room, fanning herself and screaming
in her most piercing tones:

'Now that's very kind of him! A thousand thanks! ...
How kind!' Then she disappeared and all was calm again.

Shortly before dinner the Abbé returned from Pont-
l'Évêque; as he had not heard of my intended departure,
he could not be surprised to learn I was remaining.

'Monsieur Lacase,' he said quite affably, 'I have brought
you back a few papers from Pont-l'Évêque, I am not myself
very fond of newspaper gossip, but I thought you must be
a little lacking in news here and might care to see them.'

He felt about in his cassock for them; 'Dear me! Gratien
must have taken them up to my room with my bag. Wait
a moment; I'll go and fetch them.'

'Please don't trouble, Monsieur l'Abbé,' I said, 'I will
come for them myself.'

I went up to his room with him and he invited me to
come in. While he was brushing his cassock and getting
ready for dinner, I asked him, after a few casual remarks,

whether he had known the Saint-Auréols before coming to La Quartfourche.

'No,' he said.

'Nor Monsieur Floche?' I inquired.

'I suddenly left mission-work to take up teaching. My Superior had been in communication with Monsieur Floche and he appointed me to the post I now occupy. No, before coming here I knew neither my pupil nor any of his family.'

'So that you don't know,' I asked, 'what caused Monsieur Floche to leave Paris so suddenly fifteen years ago, just as he was going to become a member of the Institut?'

'Money troubles,' he grunted.

'What! Then are Monsieur and Madame Floche living here as dependants of the Saint-Auréols?'

'Not at all, not at all!' he exclaimed impatiently; 'it is the Saint-Auréols who are ruined, or almost so. All the same La Quartfourche belongs to them, and the Floches, who are comfortably off, live with them in order to help things out; they assist in running the house and make it possible for the Saint-Auréols to keep the property, which will eventually go to Casimir. And that's about all, I think, the child will get. . . .'

'Then the daughter-in-law has no money?' I said.

'What daughter-in-law? Casimir's mother is not the daughter-in-law. She is the Saint-Auréols' own daughter.'

'But then what about the child's name?' He pretended not to understand me. 'Isn't he called Casimir de Saint-Auréol?'

'Really?' he said ironically. 'Then it is to be supposed that Mademoiselle de Saint-Auréol must have married some cousin of the same name.'

'Oh, very well,' I said, half taking his meaning and yet hesitating to draw the conclusion. He had finished brushing his cassock and, with his foot on the window-sill, was busily flicking the dust from his shoes with a handkerchief. 'And do you know her, this ... Mademoiselle de Saint-Auréol?'

'I have seen her two or three times, but she only pays flying visits here.'

'Where does she live?'

He straightened himself, flung the dusty handkerchief into a corner of the room and exclaimed:

'So it's an inquisition, is it?' ... Then, going towards his washing-stand, 'The dinner-bell will be ringing in a minute and I shan't be ready.'

It was a plain invitation for me to leave him; his pursed-up lips, I felt sure, had a deal to say, but for the moment they would let nothing more escape them.

CHAPTER FIVE

Four days later I was still at La Quartfourche, suffering less the horrid tedium of the third day, but more from fatigue. I had discovered nothing new, either from the events of each day or from my hosts' conversation. I felt my curiosity to be already dying of inanition. 'I see I must give up trying to find out anything fresh,' I thought to myself, as I once more set about preparing my departure: 'I am cut off from information on all sides; the Abbé appears to have been struck dumb ever since I have let him see how much interested I am by what he knows; the more confiding Casimir becomes, the more constrained I feel with him; I dare not question him further, and besides I now know all he can tell me – nothing more than on the day he showed me the portrait.'

Yes, one thing; the boy had very innocently let fall his mother's name. No doubt I was mad to work myself up into such a state over a flattering picture, which in all likelihood was more than fifteen years old; and even if Isabelle de Saint-Auréol were to venture on one of her fugitive appearances while I was still staying in the house, I should probably not have the power – or the courage – to put myself in her way. No matter! My thoughts had suddenly become so full of her that all my depression of spirits vanished; the last days had fled by on wings and I was astonished to find myself already at the end of the week. It had never been suggested I should stay longer at the Floches' and my work gave me no excuse for further delay, but now that the last morning had come, I spent it wandering about the park, which autumn had made more spacious and sonorous, calling upon the name of Isabelle – below my breath at first, and then aloud: Isabelle! ... and the name I had disliked at first seemed now to be fraught with elegance and rich with some clandestine charm ... Isabelle de Saint-Auréol! Isabelle! I saw her white dress flit before me round every turning of the path; every gleam of light that shone through the wavering foliage recalled her glance, her melancholy smile; and because as yet I knew nothing of love, I fancied I was in love and indulged myself in that delightful idea.

Oh, how beautiful the park was! How nobly it prepared to welcome the melancholy of the declining season! I inhaled with rapture the smell of the dank moss and rotting leaves. The great chestnut trees, whose branches swept the ground, were red and half stripped already of their leaves; some of the bushes glowed through the rain with a crimson fire; beside them the grass took on a more vivid green; a few autumn crocuses showed on the garden lawns, and lower down, in the little valley, a field was pink with them – one could see it from the quarry, where, when the rain stopped, I used to go and sit sometimes, on the same stone where I had sat with Casimir the first day – where perhaps Mademoiselle de Saint-Auréol herself had once sat and dreamed ... and I imagined myself sitting beside her.

Casimir used often to come with me, but I preferred walking by myself. Nearly every day I was caught by rain in the garden; I used to go in dripping and dry myself by the kitchen fire. Neither the cook nor Gratien liked me; my repeated advances had not succeeded in extracting half a dozen words from them. I had not been able to make friends with the dog either – however much I patted him or fed him with titbits; Terno spent the whole day lying in the huge fireplace, and whenever I came near, he growled. Casimir, whom I often used to find sitting on the edge of the hearthstone, peeling vegetables or reading, was distressed that his dog refused to treat me as a friend and would give him a reproving tap. I used often to take the book from the boy's hands and go on reading it aloud to him; he would lean up against me and I felt him listening with his whole body.

But on this particular morning, the shower that caught me was so sudden and violent that it was impossible to think of getting back to the château; I ran to the nearest shelter I could find; it was the deserted lodge you may have seen at the other end of the park near the gates; even then it had fallen into disrepair; the first room, however, was still elegantly panelled, like the drawing-room of a pleasure-lodge; but the woodwork was worm-eaten and broke away at the slightest touch. ...

When I pushed open the badly fitting door and went in, a number of bats fluttered round and then flew out of the unglazed window. I had thought it was only a passing shower, but while I stood waiting with what patience I could, the sky darkened and became completely overcast. Here I was a prisoner then, and no doubt for some time to come! It was half past ten; lunch was not till twelve. I made up my mind to wait for the first bell, which I thought I should be sure to hear from where I was; I had writing materials with me, and as I was behindhand with my correspondence, I proposed to prove to myself that an hour might be as well spent as a day. But my thoughts constantly flew back to the object of my anxious hopes and fear: oh, if I could only believe that this place would ever see her again, I would set the walls ablaze with passionate declarations! ... And then a mortal ennui, heavy with tears, slowly overwhelmed me. I sank down on the floor in a corner of the room, for there was nothing in the way of a seat, and wept like a lost child.

The word Ennui is doubtless too weak to describe the

fits of intolerable depression to which I have been subject
ever since I can remember; they overcome us suddenly;
something indefinable in the air starts them; a second
before, all was smiling, all was enjoyable; suddenly a murky
vapour rises from the depths of the soul and interposes
itself between desire and life; it forms a kind of livid screen
that separates us from the rest of the world, whose warmth,
love, colour and harmony can now only reach us as a re-
fracted, warped, transposed abstraction; we are aware of
things, but they fail to move us, and the desperate effort
to break through the screen that thus isolates our soul, might
well lead us into any sort of crime – murder, or suicide, or
madness. ...

So I dreamed, as I listened to the pouring of the rain. I
was holding in my hand the penknife I had opened in
order to sharpen my pencil, but the paper in my notebook
still remained a blank; and with the point of my knife, I
began to carve her name on a panel near by, not with much
conviction, but because I knew such was the habit of all
fond lovers; the wood was so rotten, however, that it kept
breaking away and a hole would appear instead of the
letter; I soon ceased to take any trouble; in mere idleness,
with a foolish desire for destruction, I began slashing at
random. The panel I was thus spoiling happened to be
immediately under the window; the upper part had come
away from its framework, so that the whole panel was able
to slide upwards in the side grooves. This became evident
when the pressure of my knife unexpectedly lifted it.

In a few moments, I had finished hacking the panel to
pieces; among the litter of wood there fell to the ground
an envelope; it was so stained and so mouldy, so much
the colour of the wall, that at first it gave me no shock of
astonishment; no, I was not astonished to see it; I did not
think it surprising it should be there, and so great was my

apathy that at first I made no attempt to open it. Ugly, grey, dirty, I assure you that it looked like nothing but a flake of plaster. I took it up idly; mechanically I tore it open. I pulled out two sheets covered with a large, irregular, faded handwriting, which in places, indeed, had all but disappeared. What was this letter doing here? I looked at the signature and my brain reeled; at the bottom of those pages stood the name of Isabelle!

My thoughts were so full of her. . . . For a moment I was under the illusion that it was to me she was writing:

My love, this is my last letter [she began]. Just these few words more in haste, for tonight I know I shall be unable to speak. My lips, so close to yours, will find no words but kisses. Quickly, while it is still possible, listen.

Eleven o'clock is too early; twelve will be better. You know I am dying of impatience and that waiting kills me, but we must be sure the others are asleep before I can at last waken to be yours. Yes, midnight; not before. Come to the kitchen door to meet me (you must follow the wall of the kitchen garden, where you will be in the shadow – after that, there are some bushes); wait for me there and not at the park gates, not that I am afraid of crossing the garden by myself, but the bag which I shall be taking for a few clothes will be heavy and I am not strong enough to carry it far.

And besides, it will be better for the carriage to wait at the bottom of the lane, where we shall find it easily . . . and wiser, because the farm dogs might bark and give the alarm.

No, dear love, it was impossible, you know very well, for us to have met oftener so as to arrange all this by word of mouth. You know I am a prisoner here and the old people do not allow me to go out any more than they let you come in. Ah! What a dungeon I am escaping from! . . . Yes, I will be careful to bring an extra pair of shoes with me and change into them as soon as we are in the carriage, for the grass at the bottom of the garden is sopping.

How can you ask whether I am still resolved and ready?

Why, my beloved, for months I have been preparing and holding myself ready! For years I have been living and waiting for this moment! – And whether I shall regret nothing? Don't you understand then that I have taken a loathing to everyone here who is attached to me – to everyone and everything that attaches me to this place? Is it really your gentle timid Isa who speaks so? My dear, my lover, what have you done to me, beloved? ...

This place is stifling me; I dream of the elsewhere that is opening out before me. ... I dream ... I thirst ...

I was forgetting to say that I have not been able to take the sapphires out of the case, because my aunt never leaves the keys in her room now, and none of the keys I have tried will unlock the drawer. Don't scold me; I have got Mamma's bracelet, the enamel chain, and two rings, which I don't suppose are very valuable, as she never wears them; but I think the chain is very fine. As for money, I will do what I can, but you had better get some too.

Yours, with all my prayers. Soon, soon to meet!

Your
ISA

Dated this twenty-second day of October, my twenty-second birthday and the eve of my flight.

I think with terror of all the stuff I should have to spin out here, if I had to cook this story up into a novel – four or five pages at least of reflections after reading the letter, interrogations, perplexities. ... In reality, as is the case after any very violent shock, I fell into a state of semi-lethargy. When at last, through the confused rushing of blood in my brain, I heard the sound of a bell, which was repeated – 'Heavens!' thought I to myself, 'it's the second luncheon bell! How can I have missed hearing the first?' I pulled out my watch. Twelve o'clock! I dashed out instantly with the glowing letter pressed to my heart, and darted back to the house, bareheaded, through the rain.

The Floches were already wondering anxiously what had become of me, and when I appeared panting:

'Why, dear Monsieur Lacase, you are drenched,' they cried, 'absolutely drenched!'

Then they declared no one should sit down to table until I had changed my clothes; and as soon as I came down they began to question me with kind solicitude; I had to explain that I had taken shelter in the lodge and had waited in vain for a break in the shower; then they apologized for the bad weather, for the shocking state of the paths, for the second bell, which had certainly been rung too soon, for the first, which had not been rung as loud as usual. . . . Mademoiselle Verdure went to fetch a shawl, which they implored me to put round my shoulders, because I was still over-heated and might catch cold. The Abbé meanwhile was watching me, with his lips screwed up into a regular grimace, and so nervous was I under his searching glance, that I felt myself blush and grow as uneasy as a child who has been caught out in a misdemeanour. 'But it is essential for me to get round him,' I thought, 'for he is now the only person from whom it will be possible to learn anything – the only person who may cast some light on the intricacies of this dark and mysterious affair, which I am bent on exploring now more out of love than curiosity.' After coffee, the cigarette I offered the Abbé served as an excuse for a private conversation; we went to smoke in the orangery, in order not to incommode the Baronne.

'I thought you were only going to stop here a week,' he began in an ironical voice.

'I was not counting on such kind hosts.'

'Then Monsieur Floche's documents . . . ?'

'Are assimilated. . . . But I have found other things that interest me more.'

I expected a question, but none came.

'You must know the secrets of this château inside out,' I went on impatiently.

He opened his eyes wide, wrinkled his brows, and put on an air of stupid candour.

'Why is Madame or Mademoiselle de Saint-Auréol, your pupil's mother, not here with us, engaged in looking after her afflicted son and her aged parents?'

In order better to feign astonishment, he threw away his cigarette and opened his hands in a parenthesis on each side of his face.

'No doubt her occupations detain her elsewhere ...' he muttered. 'What an insidious question!'

'Do you want one that is more to the point? What did Madame or Mademoiselle de Saint-Auréol, your pupil's mother, do on a certain October 22nd, the night fixed for her to run away with her lover?'

He struck an attitude, with his hands on his hips:

'Oh ho! oh ho! my young novelist!' (I had been vain or weak enough some time previously to confide in him the kind of thing that should never be spoken of except in cases of deep personal sympathy; and since he had become aware of my proclivities he had taken to laughing at me in a way I was beginning to find intolerable.) – 'Aren't you going a little fast? ... And may I ask you in my turn how you come to know so much?'

'Because the letter Isabelle de Saint-Auréol wrote to her lover that day did not fall into his hands but into mine.'

Decidedly I was a person to be reckoned with: just at that moment the Abbé discovered a little spot on the sleeve of his cassock and began scratching it with his finger-nail; he was coming to terms.

'There is one thing that surprises me,' he said, 'that as soon as a person considers himself a born novelist, he thinks he has a right to do anything he pleases. Anybody else would think twice before reading a letter that was not addressed to him.'

'I hope, Monsieur l'Abbé, he would not read it at all.'

I looked at him steadily, but he kept on scratching with his eyes down.

'I hardly suppose though that anyone gave it you to read.'

'The letter fell into my hands accidentally; the envelope was old, dirty, half torn, and without a trace of writing on it; when I opened it, I saw it was a letter from Mademoiselle de Saint-Auréol; but addressed to whom? ... Come now, Monsieur l'Abbé, help me; who was Mademoiselle de Saint-Auréol's lover fourteen years ago?'

The Abbé had risen; he began to walk up and down, his head lowered, his hands crossed behind his back; as he passed behind my chair, he stopped; and I suddenly felt his hands alight heavily on my shoulders:

'Show me that letter.'

'Will you speak then?'

I felt his grasp quivering with impatience.

'Oh, no conditions, I beg. Show me the letter. That's enough.'

'Let me go and fetch it,' I said, trying to free myself.

'You have it there, in your pocket.'

He fixed his eyes on the right spot, as if my coat had been transparent. Hang it all! He could hardly be going to search me! ...

I was in a very bad posture for defending myself, and against a great strapping fellow too, who was stronger than I; and what means should I have afterwards of making him speak? I turned round and saw his face almost touching mine – a swollen, red, apoplectic face, with two great veins starting out on the forehead and ugly pockets under the eyes. Then, forcing myself to laugh, for fear of things going altogether wrong:

'Gracious goodness, Abbé, you must confess you know something of curiosity yourself!'

He let go his hold; I rose at once and made as though to leave the room.

'If you had not behaved yourself so like a brigand, I should have shown it to you long ago.' Then, taking his arm: 'But let's go nearer the drawing-room, so that I may call for help, if necessary.'

By a great effort of will I kept up a joking manner, but my heart was beating fast.

'There! read it before me,' I said, taking the letter from my pocket, 'I want to see what kind of face an Abbé makes when he reads a love-letter.'

But he had recovered control of himself and only showed his agitation by the irrepressible twitching of a little muscle in his cheek. He read the letter, then smelt the paper, frowning severely as he sniffed, so that his eyes seemed to be reproving the greediness of his nose; then folding the paper up again, he returned it to me, and said somewhat solemnly:

'On that same 22nd of October, Viscount Blaise de Gonfreville perished in a hunting accident.'

'You make my blood run cold!' (My imagination at once built up an appalling drama.) 'You must know that I found the letter behind a panel in the lodge, from which place he was certainly meant to fetch it.'

The Abbé then told me that young Gonfreville, the eldest son of a family whose estate bordered upon the Saint-Auréols', had been found dead beside a gate he had apparently been intending to climb, when a clumsy movement had made his gun go off. No cartridge, however, had been found in the barrel of his gun. Not a soul could give any information about the accident; the young man had gone out alone without being seen by anyone; but the next day one of the La Quartfourche dogs had been found licking a pool of blood.

'I was not at La Quartfourche at the time,' continued he, 'but from what I afterwards learnt, it seems to me certain that the crime was committed by Gratien, who had no doubt discovered his young mistress's relations with the Viscount and had perhaps heard of her proposed flight (which I myself knew nothing of before reading this letter); he is a rough, dogged fellow – vindictive too, perhaps – an old servant who, if it came to the point, might very well think he need stick at nothing in defence of his masters' property.'

'Why was he not arrested?'

'It was to nobody's interest to prosecute him, and the two families of Gonfreville and Saint-Auréol were equally anxious to hush up this unfortunate affair; for a few months later, Mademoiselle de Saint-Auréol gave birth to a wretched little child. Casimir's deformity is attributed to the pains his mother took to hide her condition; but God teaches us that the sins of the fathers are often visited on the children. Come with me to the lodge; I am curious to see the place where you found the letter.'

The sky had cleared and we set out together.

Everything went smoothly on our way to the lodge; the Abbé took my arm and we walked in step together, talking amicably. But on the way back it was another matter. No doubt we were both somewhat excited by the strangeness of the adventure; but each of us in a very different manner. Quickly disarmed by the smiling and obliging way with which the Abbé had finally told me what he knew, I forgot his cloth and my own reserve and found myself speaking to him as man to man. ... This, I think, is how the quarrel began:

'Who will tell us,' said I, 'what Mademoiselle de Saint-Auréol did that night? Did she wait for him in the garden? And for how long? What were her thoughts when she saw he was not coming?'

The Abbé, absolutely unmoved by my psychological flights, remained silent.

'Think of the delicate young girl, her heart heavy with love and discontent, her head full of wild fancies – think of the passionate Isabelle ...'

'The shameless Isabelle,' muttered the Abbé below his breath.

I continued as if I had not heard him, but in my growing excitement I was already preparing to answer his next interjection.

'Think,' I exclaimed, 'of all the hope and all the despair that must ...'

'Why think of all that?' he interrupted sharply. 'It is not our business to know more about events than that part of them that may serve to instruct us.'

'But according as we know more or less, they will instruct us differently. ...'

'What do you mean?'

'That the superficial knowledge of events does not always, nor indeed often, concord with the deeper knowledge which we may gain of them later, and that the instruction they then bring with them will not be the same; that it is a good thing to inquire before drawing conclusions. ...'

'Take care, my young friend, take care! There is a germ of revolt lying in the spirit of inquiry and critical curiosity. The great man you have chosen for your model should have shown you ...'

'The great man I have chosen to write my thesis on, you mean. ...'

'What a hair-splitter you are! That is the spirit which ...'

'But really, my dear Abbé, I should like to know whether it wasn't that selfsame spirit of curiosity which made you come with me just now to the lodge, which made you hang for several moments over a broken panel, and which has gradually driven you to find out all the details of the story you have just told me! ...'

His step became more agitated, his voice sharper; he tapped the ground impatiently with his stick.

'I don't look for explanations of explanations like you. I go no further than the fact itself. The lamentable occurrences I have acquainted you with would teach me, if I still needed teaching, to look on carnal sin with horror; I find here the condemnation of divorce and of all men's contrivances for palliating the consequences of their offences. That is surely sufficient!'

'No, not for me. I care nothing for the fact, so long as I cannot discover its cause. To learn Isabelle de Saint-Auréol's secret life, to trace out the perfumed paths she trod, their pathos, their darkness ...'

'Take care, young man! You are falling in love with her!'

'Ah! I was expecting that! Because I am not satisfied with appearances, because words do not blind me – nor acts neither. ... Are you sure you are not judging her unfairly?'

'The trollop!'

I grew hot with indignation. It was with the greatest difficulty that I controlled myself.

'Monsieur l'Abbé, such words surprise me in your mouth. I thought that Christ had taught us to forgive, not to chastise.'

'There is but one step from indulgence to encouragement.'

'*He* at any rate would not have condemned her as you do.'

'In the first place, what do you know about that? In the

second place, He who is without sin Himself may show more indulgence towards the sins of others than ... I mean, it is not the business of us sinners to find more or less excuse for sin, but simply to turn aside from it with horror.'

'After having first taken a good sniff at it, as you did at the letter!'

'Impertinence!' And abruptly breaking away from me, he darted off down a little side path, flinging biting words behind him, like Parthian shots; I could only make out a few of them: 'Modern education! ... Sophist! ... Anarchist! ...'

When we met again at dinner, he still looked frowningly, but as we left the table, he came up to me with a smile and put out his hand, which I took with a smile too.

The evening seemed to me more dismal even than usual. The Baron groaned softly by the fireside. Monsieur Floche and the Abbé moved their draughtsmen without a word. I saw Casimir out of the corner of my eye, with his head buried in his hands, slowly slobbering on to his book and from time to time mopping it with his handkerchief. I gave only just sufficient attention to the game of bezique to prevent my partner from being too ignominiously beaten; Madame Floche noticed my dullness and tried anxiously to make the game a little more lively:

'Now then, Olympe! It's your turn. Are you asleep?'

No, it was not sleep but death that was benumbing my hosts with its grim and icy touch. I myself felt a mortal anguish – a kind of horror – seize me. Oh spring! Oh gusts of heaven, perfumes and delights and aery music, never more will you be wafted here! So I dreamed; and I thought of you, Isabelle! What of the tomb you escaped from? What of the life you fled to? I imagined you sitting there – there, in the peaceful lamplight, your pale forehead drooping on your delicate fingers, a curl of black hair touching – caressing – your wrist. What a far-away look is in your eyes! That sigh the others do not hear – what nameless weariness of flesh and spirit does it tell of so plaintively? And I myself unconsciously heaved a huge sigh, which was partly a yawn and partly a sob, so that Madame de Saint-Auréol, throwing her last trump on to the table, exclaimed:

'I think Monsieur Lacase is badly wanting to go off to bed.'

Poor lady!

That night I had an absurd dream – a dream which at first was merely a continuation of the reality.

The evening was not over; I was still in the drawing-room with my hosts; but a set of people were there too whose numbers were continually increasing, though I never actually saw anyone come into the room; I recognized Casimir sitting at a game of patience over which three or four persons were bending. Everyone was talking in whispers, so that at first I could not make out any actual words, but I realized that everyone present was pointing out something extraordinary to his neighbour, who in his turn showed astonishment; they were all looking at one particular point, just beside Casimir, and I suddenly saw that there, at that very table, was seated – how had I not noticed her before? – Isabelle de Saint-Auréol. She alone, amongst all the other persons in dark clothes, was dressed in white. At first I thought she looked charming, not unlike her portrait in the locket; but after a moment I was struck by the immobility of her features, the fixity of her stare, and I suddenly understood what was being whispered all about me: it was not the real Isabelle who was there, but a doll got up to look like her, which had been put in her place during the real one's absence. This doll, I thought, was frightful;

its air of pretentious stupidity got painfully on my nerves; it seemed to be motionless, but as I looked at it attentively, I saw it slowly bend over to one side – lower – lower ... it was on the point of toppling over, when Mademoiselle Olympe, rushing up from the other end of the drawing-room, stooped down to the ground, lifted the arm-chair's loose cover, and began winding up some sort of oddly creaking machinery which righted the figure again, and at the same time set its arms working with the grotesque gestures of an automaton. Everyone then got up, the hour for departure having struck; the false Isabelle was to be left there by herself; on going out everyone saluted her with a Turkish salaam, except the Baron, who went up to her and irreverently seizing her wig with his hand planted two smacking kisses on her sinciput, chuckling as he did so. As soon as the company had all left the drawing-room – and I saw crowds go out – as soon as it was quite dark, I saw – yes, in the dark – I saw the doll turn pale, quiver, come to life. She rose slowly and it was Mademoiselle de Saint-Auréol herself: she glided towards me noiselessly; suddenly I felt her soft arms round my neck, and I woke up in the warm moisture of her breath, just as she was saying tenderly:

'For all the others I am absent – for you only do I come.'

I am neither superstitious nor nervous; if I lighted my candle, it was in order to banish this haunting image from my eyes and mind; I found it difficult. In spite of myself, I listened to every sound. Suppose she were really to come! In vain I endeavoured to read; I could fix my attention on nothing else; I was still thinking of her when in the early morning I fell asleep.

CHAPTER SIX

AND so the ups and downs of my love-sick curiosity flared and flickered. It was impossible, however, to put off my departure – which I had again announced – any longer, and this was my last day at La Quartfourche. It was on this day that ...

Imagine us sitting at lunch, waiting for the post, which Gratien's wife, Delphine, usually brings in a little before dessert. It is first taken, as I have said before, to Madame Floche, who sorts out the letters and hands Monsieur Floche the *Journal des débats*, behind which he disappears until we leave the table. This morning, a mauve envelope, which has accidentally caught in the wrapper of the paper, suddenly drops out and flies across the table towards Madame Floche's plate. I have just time to recognize the large straggling writing which had already made my heart beat the day before. Madame Floche apparently recognizes it too; she makes a hasty effort to cover the envelope with her plate; the plate knocks against a glass and breaks it, spilling the wine all over the table-cloth. In the turmoil that follows good Madame Floche, taking advantage of the general confusion, succeeds in spiriting away the envelope and concealing it under her mitten.

'I was trying to kill a spider,' she says awkwardly, like a child excusing herself. (Whatever insect happens to come out of the fruit dishes, she always calls a spider – it is no matter to her whether it is really a woodlouse or an earwig.)

'And I'll wager you missed it,' says Madame de Saint-Auréol acidly, getting up and throwing her napkin on to the table unfolded. 'Please come to me in the drawing-room, Sister. The gentlemen will excuse me. I've got my stomach cramps again.'

The meal comes to an end in silence. Monsieur Floche has seen nothing, and Monsieur de Saint-Auréol understood nothing. Mademoiselle Verdure and the Abbé sit with their eyes fixed on their plates; if Casimir weren't blowing his nose, I should think he was crying.....

The weather this morning is almost warm, and coffee is served on the little terrace outside the drawing-room windows. I am the only person to take it with Mademoiselle Verdure and the Abbé; from the drawing-room, where the two ladies are shut up together, can be heard an occasional outburst of voices; then silence; the ladies have gone upstairs.

It was at this moment, if I remember right, that the engagement of the parsley-leaved beech took place.

Mademoiselle Verdure and the Abbé lived in a continual state of warfare. Their battles were not very serious and merely amused the Abbé; nothing, however, irritated Mademoiselle Verdure more than the derisive tone adopted by him on these occasions; she came out into the open at every shot and the Abbé fired his volleys point-blank. Hardly a day passed without one of these skirmishes, referred to by the Abbé as 'engagements'. He used to declare they were good for the old maid's health and he would set to work to get a rise out of her just as one takes a dog out for its daily walk. It was done perhaps without unkindness – but certainly not without a spice of malice, and he could be not a little provoking. It gave them both something to do and added a flavour to their day.

We had all been somewhat upset by the little incident at dessert and I cast about in search of some diversion.

While the Abbé was pouring out the coffee, I put my hand into my pocket and came upon a little bunch of leaves – a twig I had that morning broken off a curious tree which grew by the park gate. I had meant to ask Mademoiselle Verdure its name, not so much out of curiosity to know it, as because it flattered her to have an appeal made to her learning.

For she loved botanizing. Now and then she would start out for the day to collect specimens, looking somewhat absurd, with a green box slung across her sturdy shoulders; and all the hours she could spare from her domestic cares were divided between her dried plants and her magnifying glass. ... Mademoiselle Olympe, therefore, took the twig and without a moment's hesitation, pronounced it to be parsley-leaved beech.

'What a queer name,' said I doubtfully; 'one can hardly imagine these lanceolate leaves having any connexion with ...'

The Abbé, who had been smiling significantly for the last minute or two, now observed carelessly:

'That is the name they give the *fagus persicifolia* at La Quartfourche.'

Mademoiselle Verdure positively jumped:

'I didn't know you were so good at botany, Monsieur l'Abbé,' she said.

'No, perhaps not,' he said, 'but I happen to know a little Latin.' He turned to me: 'These poor ladies are the victims of an unintentional pun. *Persicus*, my dear lady,' he went on, '*persicus* means *peach tree* – not *parsley*.* The *fagus persicifolia*, whose leaves Monsieur Lacase has noticed and so correctly called lanceolate – the *fagus persicifolia* is a *peach*-leaved beech tree.'

Mademoiselle Olympe had turned crimson; the affected

* *Persil* in French.

unconcern of the Abbé put the final touch to her discomfiture.

'True botany has nothing to do with anomalies and monstrosities,' was all she managed to get out, and without another look at the Abbé, she emptied her cup at one gulp and flounced off.

The Abbé had screwed up his mouth till it looked like the hinder end of a hen, and was letting off a series of small explosions. It was with the greatest difficulty that I kept from laughing.

'Monsieur l'Abbé,' I said, 'I'm afraid you're a wicked man!'

'Not at all! Not at all! ... The good lady doesn't take enough exercise; she wants stirring up now and then. She's very pugnacious, believe me; if I let her go three days without a taste of my steel, she comes thrusting at me herself. There are not so many amusements at La Quartfourche, you know ...!'

And then without a word being said on either side, we began to think of the letter at the luncheon table.

'Did you recognize the handwriting?' I ventured to ask at last.

He shrugged his shoulders:

'A little sooner or a little later, it's the letter that comes to La Quartfourche twice a year, after rent-day, and in which she announces her arrival to Madame Floche.'

'She is coming then?' I cried.

'Now, now, keep calm; you won't see her.'

'And why shouldn't I see her?'

'Because she arrives in the middle of the night and goes away again almost at once – because she doesn't want to be seen by anyone and ... beware of Gratien.'

He gave me a searching look, but I did not move a muscle and he continued with some irritation:

'You won't pay any attention to what I say – I can see it by your look; anyhow you've been warned. Well, go on! Do as you please; tomorrow morning you shall tell me all about it.'

He got up and went away, leaving me unable to make out whether he had meant to check my curiosity or whether he had not been amusing himself on the contrary by prodding it up.

Until evening came my mind, in a state of confusion I cannot attempt to describe, was solely occupied by waiting for the moments to pass. Was I really in love with Isabelle? Doubtless not. But how could I have failed to think so when, stirred to the very heart by the violence of my excitement, I recognized in my curiosity all the symptoms of love – its quivering ardour, its impetuosity, its impatience? The Abbé's last words had only made me keener. What harm could Gratien do me? I was prepared to go through fire and water!

There was certainly something unusual brewing. That evening no one suggested a game. Directly after supper Madame de Saint-Auréol began to complain of her 'gasteritis', as she called it, and retired without further excuse, while Mademoiselle Verdure prepared her a hot drink. A few minutes later, Madame Floche sent Casimir to bed, and as soon as he was gone, said:

'I believe Monsieur Lacase would very much like to follow suit; he looks dead with sleep.'

And as I did not at once act on the hint, she added:

'I don't think any of us are inclined to sit up late.'

Mademoiselle Verdure got up to light the candles; the Abbé and I followed her; I saw Madame Floche bend over her husband who was dozing in the *berline* by the fire; he rose at once, and taking the Baron by the arm, he dragged him off unresisting and as if he understood what was wanted of him. On the landing, where everyone, candlestick in hand, went off each in his own direction, the Abbé wished me good night:

'Sleep well,' said he with a meaning smile.

I shut the door of my room and then I waited. It was only nine o'clock. I heard Madame Floche come up and then Mademoiselle Verdure. There was the continuation of a rather lively quarrel on the landing between Madame Floche and Madame de Saint-Auréol, who had come out of her room again, but they were too far off for me to catch any words. Then a sound of doors slamming; then nothing more.

I stretched myself on my bed the better to reflect. I thought of the Abbé's ironical hope that I should sleep well when he wished me good night; I should have liked to know whether he himself was preparing for sleep or whether he would now indulge the curiosity he would not allow himself to show in my presence. But his room was in another part of the house, in the opposite wing to that in which I slept, and no plausible motive could justify my presence there. Yet which of us two, I wondered, if we were to meet in the passage, would look the greater fool? ... Meditating thus, I was overtaken by an inexcusable, an absurd, an amazing circumstance – I fell asleep.

Yes, less excited, no doubt, than exhausted by my long hours of suspense, worn out too by my nightmare of the evening before, I fell into a deep sleep.

The sputtering of my dying candle woke me – or perhaps it was some faint vibration of the floor which I had been vaguely conscious of during my sleep; certainly there had been steps in the passage. I sat up. At the same moment my candle went out; there I was in the dark, in a state of utter bewilderment. I had nothing to see by but a few matches; I struck one to look at my watch – it was almost half past eleven; I strained my ears – not a sound. I groped my way to the door and opened it.

No, my heart was not beating; I felt buoyant and alert in body; calm, wary and determined in mind.

At the other end of the passage, a glimmer of light streamed in on me from a large window; it did not shine steadily as in still nights, but flickered and at times died fitfully away, for the sky was overcast and the wind was driving heavy clouds across the moon. I had taken off my shoes and advanced noiselessly. ... It was not too dark for me to find my way to the observation post I had arranged for myself in a little unused room next to Madame Floche's, where I supposed the confabulation would take place! (it had at one time been occupied by Monsieur Floche, but he now preferred the neighbourhood of his books to that of his wife). The door of communication, which I had carefully bolted in order to guard against surprises, had dropped a little, leaving a gap under the frame at the top, through which I found it was possible to see; to reach this I had to perch myself on the top of a chest of drawers which I had pushed close up to the spot.

A ray of light now shone through this gap and, reflected from the white ceiling, enabled me to see my way. Everything was exactly as I had left it the day before. I climbed on to the chest of drawers and peered down into the next room. ...

Isabelle de Saint-Auréol was there.

I saw her before me, only a few paces away. ... She was sitting on one of those low seats – ugly things without backs, called, I believe, 'poufs' – which it gave me something of a shock to see in this ancient room, and which I did not remember noticing the day I took in the flowers. Madame Floche was buried in a great tapestry-covered arm-chair; on a little table at her side stood a lamp which

cast a subdued light over them both. Isabelle had her back
to me; she was leaning forward – almost lying across her
old aunt's lap, so that at first I could not see her face. Before
long, however, she raised her head. She had aged less than
I expected, but I could scarcely recognize the young girl
of the miniature; her beauty certainly was not less, but it
was a beauty of a very different kind – more earthly, grown
more human, as it were. The angelic candour of the portrait
had given way to a passionate languor; the corners of her
mouth, which the artist had drawn half open, were now
curled in an indefinable expression of discontent. A large
travelling cloak, a sort of waterproof, made, so it seemed,
of some rather cheap material, covered her dress almost
entirely, except where it was a little hitched up and showed
a skirt of shiny black silk, against which her ungloved hand,
holding a crumpled handkerchief, hung down looking
extraordinarily white and fragile. On her head she wore
a little befeathered bonnet with silk strings, from under
which a curl of very black hair had escaped and fell over
her temple whenever she leaned forward. One might have
thought her in mourning but for a brilliant beetle-green
ribbon she wore round her neck. Neither she nor Madame
Floche were speaking; but Isabelle with her right hand was
gently stroking Madame Floche's arm, and then she drew
her hand towards her and covered it with kisses.

And now she was shaking her head while her curls waved
from left to right; at last she said, as though in repetition of
some previous statement: 'Everything – I have really tried
everything. I swear . . .'

'Don't swear, my poor child; I believe you without that,'
interrupted the poor old lady, putting her hand on Isabelle's
head. They both spoke very low, as if afraid of being over-
heard.

At last Madame Floche raised herself gently, pushed away

her niece and, helping herself up by its arms, rose from her chair. Mademoiselle de Saint-Auréol got up at the same time and followed her aunt for a few steps towards the writing-table from which Casimir had taken the miniature two days before. She stopped in front of a console-table, on which stood a great mirror, and, while the old lady was fumbling in a drawer, caught sight in the glass of the emerald ribbon she was wearing round her neck; quickly unfastening it, she wound it round her finger, and before Madame Floche turned round the bright ribbon had vanished and Isabelle had taken up a pensive attitude, her hands crossed on her knees, her eyes gazing into space. ...

Madame Floche, poor old thing, was still holding her bunch of keys in one hand and in the other the meagre little bundle of notes she had taken out of the drawer; she was just going to seat herself again in her arm-chair, when the door opposite that at which I was posted was suddenly flung open – and I could hardly restrain a cry of stupefaction. The Baronne was standing stiffly in the doorway, *décolletée*, rouged, in full ceremonial attire and her head surmounted by what looked like a gigantic feather brush of marabout. She was staggering under the weight of a great six-branched candelabra in which all the candles were burning, flooding her with their flickering light and shedding tears of wax all over the floor. She had come, no doubt, to the end of her strength, for she began by hastily making for the table and setting down the candelabra in front of the looking-glass; then, taking four skips back to her position in the doorway, she once more advanced, solemnly and with measured steps, stretching out at full length in front of her a hand loaded with enormous rings. In the middle of the room, she stood still, turned stiffly towards her daughter and, with hand outstretched, shrieked in ear-splitting accents:

'Get thee behind me, ungrateful daughter! Your tears

can no longer move me and your protestations have for ever lost the way to my heart.'

The whole speech was delivered with no variation of tone at the topmost pitch of her voice. In the meantime, Isabelle had thrown herself at her mother's feet and taken hold of her dress; as she pulled it to one side, revealing two absurd little white satin slippers, she herself continued to strike her forehead on the floor, where a rug was spread over the boards. Madame de Saint-Auréol did not lower her eyes for an instant; still looking straight before her, with glances as piercing and icy as her voice, she continued:

'Is it not enough for you to have brought poverty into the dwelling of your parents? Are you contemplating a further ...'

Here her voice suddenly failed her and she turned towards Madame Floche, who, making herself as small as she could, sat trembling in her arm-chair:

'And as for you, Sister, if you are still so weak ...' (she took herself up) 'if you are still so unpardonably weak as to yield to her entreaties, even for one kiss – even for one groat – so true as I am your elder sister, I leave you – I recommend my household gods to Heaven, and I leave you, never to set eyes on you again.'

I seemed to be looking on at a play. But since they were unconscious of being watched, for whose benefit was it these two marionettes were acting this tragedy? The attitudes and gestures of the daughter seemed to me as exaggerated and as artificial as those of the mother. ... The latter was facing me, so that I saw Isabelle from behind, still prostrate in the posture of a suppliant Esther; all at once I caught sight of her feet; the boots she wore, as far as I could see through the coating of mud that covered them, seemed to have tops of puce-coloured *poult-de-soie*; above them showed her white stockings, across which the dripping, muddy flounce of her lifted skirt had left a smear of dirt. .... And instantly the long story of adventure and wretchedness told by these poor witnesses spoke more loudly to my heart than all the old woman's declamatory tirades. A sob rose in my throat; I made up my mind to follow Isa through the garden when she left the house.

In the meantime Madame de Saint-Auréol had taken three steps towards Madame Floche's chair:

'Come, give me up those notes. Do you imagine I do not see the paper you are crumpling in your hand? Do you think me blind or mad? Give me the money, I tell you!' And seizing the notes, she held them melodramatically to the flame of one of the candles in the candelabra: 'I would rather burn them all' (needless to say, she did nothing of the sort) 'than let her have a groat.'

She slipped the notes into her pocket and resumed her theatrical attitude:

'Ungrateful daughter! Unnatural daughter! My bracelets and my necklaces, you know what road they took! Let my rings go the same way!'

So saying, with a dexterous movement of her outstretched hand, she let two or three drop on the floor. Like a famished dog after a bone, Isabelle flung herself upon them.

'Now go! We have nothing more to say to each other; I no longer acknowledge you.'

Then, having fetched an extinguisher from the bed-table, she extinguished one after the other all the candles in the candelabra and departed.

The room now seemed dark. Isabelle in the meantime had got up; she passed her fingers across her forehead, threw back her scattered curls and adjusted her bonnet. With a swift shake she jerked up her cloak, which had slipped a little off her shoulders, and bent over Madame

Floche to wish her good-bye. The poor woman seemed trying to speak to her, but her voice was too weak for me to make out what she said. Isabelle silently pressed one of the old woman's trembling hands to her lips. An instant after I darted in pursuit of her down the passage.

Just as I reached the stairs, I was arrested by the sound of voices and recognized one of them as Mademoiselle Verdure's. Isabelle had already come upon her in the hall, and by leaning over the banisters, I could see them both. Olympe Verdure had a little lantern in her hand.

'Are you going away without giving him a kiss?' she said and I understood they were talking of Casimir. 'Don't you want to see him then?'

'No, Loly, I'm too much in a hurry. Don't let him know I've been here.'

There was silence – something was going on in dumbshow which I couldn't at first make out. The lantern was moving about and cast leaping shadows; Mademoiselle Verdure advancing, Isabelle retreating, both of them had moved a few steps from their original positions; then I heard:

'Yes, yes; in remembrance of me. I've been keeping it such a long time. Now I'm old, what use would it be to me?'

'Loly! Loly! Of all I'm leaving here there's no one as good as you.'

Mademoiselle Verdure put her arms round her :

'Oh, poor darling! How wet she is!'

'Only my cloak – it's nothing. Let me go now.'

'Take an umbrella then.'

'It has stopped raining.'

'The lantern.'

'No. I don't want it. The carriage is quite close. Good-bye.'

'Well then, good-bye, my poor child. May God ...' She ended with a sob. Mademoiselle Verdure stayed for a few moments leaning out into the night, and a draught of damp air blew in from outside up the well of the staircase; then I heard her close the door and bolt it.

I could not get past Mademoiselle Verdure. The key of the kitchen door was removed every night by Gratien. True, there was another door on·the other side of the house by which I could easily have got out, but it was an immense way round; before I could have found her, Isabelle would have already got to her carriage. Ha! supposing I called her from my window? ... I hurried back to my room. The moon was again obscured; I caught the sound of footsteps and waited a moment. A violent gust of wind arose and, as Gratien went in by the kitchen, I heard, through the whispering of the storm-tossed trees, the wheels of the carriage that bore away Isabelle de Saint-Auréol.

CHAPTER SEVEN

I HAD delayed over-long, and as soon as I got back to Paris I was beset by a thousand preoccupations which turned my thoughts at length into other channels. The resolution I had made of returning to La Quartfourche the following summer lessened my regrets at not having been able to carry my adventure further. I was indeed beginning to forget it, when towards the end of January I received a formal announcement of the deaths of Monsieur and Madame Floche. The two old people had resigned their gentle tremulous souls into their Maker's hands within a few days of one another. I recognized Mademoiselle Verdure's handwriting on the envelope; but it was to Casimir I wrote the banal expression of my regret and sympathy. Two weeks later I received the following letter:

MY DEAR MONSIEUR GÉRARD,

[*The child had always refused to call me by my surname.*

'*What is your name?*' *he had asked me during one of our walks.*

'*Why, you know it already, Casimir; I am called Monsieur Lacase.*'

'*No; not that name – the other?*' *he had insisted.*]

It is very kind of you to have written me such a nice letter. I liked it very much. La Quartfourche is very sad now. My grandmother had a stroke on Thursday and was obliged to keep her room; then Mamma came back to La Quartfourche and the Abbé went away, because he was made curé at Breuil. Then, after that, my uncle and aunt died. First uncle died. He was very fond of you, you know. And then the Sunday after that, aunt. She was ill for three days. Mamma had gone away. I was all alone with Loly and Delphine – Gratien's wife; she is very fond of me. And it was very sad because aunt didn't want to leave me. But it couldn't be helped. And now I sleep in the room next Delphine's, because Loly had to go to her brother-in-law's in the Orne. Gratien is very kind to me too. He has shown me how to make cuttings and grafts, and it is very amusing. And I am helping cut down the trees too.

You know the little paper that you wrote your promise on. You must forget it, because there's no one here now for you to stay with. But I am very sorry to think I shan't see you again, because I was very fond of you. But I haven't forgotten you.

Your little friend,

CASIMIR

Monsieur and Madame Floche's death had left me more or less indifferent, but this awkward, artless letter touched me. I was not free at the moment, but I determined to make an expedition of inquiry to La Quartfourche as soon as the Easter holidays came round. What did it matter to me that there was no one for me to stay with? I could put up at Pont-l'Évêque and hire a carriage from there. Need I add that the thought of a possible meeting with the mysterious Isabelle was as great an attraction as my deep pity for the poor child? There were passages in his letter which were incomprehensible; it was difficult to link the facts together. ... The old lady's stroke, Isabelle's arrival, the Abbé's departure, the death of the old Floches, Isabelle's absence at the time, the departure of Mademoiselle Verdure ... were these a merely fortuitous series of events, or was there some connexion between them? Casimir could not and the Abbé would not enlighten me. There was nothing for it but to wait till April. On the second day of my holidays I started.

At Breuil station, I caught sight of the Abbé just as he was getting into my train; I hailed him.

'So here you are back again,' said he.

'Yes; as a matter of fact, I didn't think I should be returning so soon.'

He got into my compartment. We were alone.

'Well. There have been changes here since you left.'

'Yes; I heard you had become curé at Breuil.'

'Oh, I didn't mean that,' and he made a gesture with his outspread hand which I remembered. 'Did you get an announcement?'

'Yes; and I at once wrote a letter of condolence to your pupil. It was he who told me some of the news; but he wasn't very explicit. I very nearly wrote and asked you for details.'

'You should have done so.'

'I thought it wouldn't be very easy to get them out of you,' I answered, laughing.

But the Abbé no doubt felt less necessity for discretion than when he was staying at La Quartfourche, and seemed inclined to talk.

'It's a wretched state of affairs, isn't it?' said he. 'There's an end of the woods.'

At first I did not understand; then a sentence of Casimir's letter came back to my mind: 'I am helping to cut down the trees . . .'

'What are they doing that for?' I asked ingenuously.

'What for, my good sir? Go and ask the creditors: but after all it's not their work; it's all being done behind their backs. The place is mortgaged up to the hilt. Mademoiselle de Saint-Auréol is making off with as much as she can.'

'Is she there?'

'As if you didn't know!'

'I merely guessed it from a few words that . . .'

'It's since she came back that everything has gone to the dogs.'

153

He caught himself up for a moment, but this time the desire to speak was too much for him; he did not even wait for me to question him and I thought it wiser not to; he went on:

'How came she to hear of her mother's stroke? I never made out. When she learnt that the old Baronne couldn't leave her chair, in she marched with all her baggage, and Madame Floche hadn't the heart to turn her out. It was after that that I went away.'

'It was very sad your leaving Casimir like that.'

'Possibly, but it was not my place to stay in the same house with a shameless ... But I forgot you stood up for her.'

'I shall very likely continue to do so, Monsieur le Curé.'

'Very good. Very good. Yes, I know; Mademoiselle Verdure stood up for her too. She stood up for her until the day the old folk died.'

I was amused to notice that the Abbé had almost entirely dropped the elegant language he had favoured while he was at La Quartfourche, and had adopted the speech and manners peculiar to the curés of Normandy villages. He went on with his train of thought:

'She thought it odd too when they died so soon one after the other.'

'Did they ...?'

'I say nothing,' and he pursed up his lips in his old way, but immediately started off again:

'All the same there was a good deal of gossip in the neighbourhood. People weren't pleased to see the niece come into the property. And you see even Verdure thought it best to leave too.'

'Who looks after Casimir?'

'Ah! even you understand that his mother is not a proper person to be with the child. He spends nearly the whole of his time with the Chointreuils – you know – the gardener and his wife.'

'Gratien?'

'Yes, Gratien; he tried to prevent the park trees from being cut down; but there was nothing to be done. It's simply ruin.'

'But surely the Floches had money?'

'Oh, that all went the first day, my dear sir. Two of the three farms on the estate belonged to Madame Floche, but it's many a long day since they were bought up by the tenants. The third, the little farm of Les Fonds, still belongs to the Baronne; there was no tenant and Gratien ran it; but it will be put up for sale with the rest.'

'La Quartfourche is to be put up for sale?'

'By auction. But it can't be done before the end of the summer. In the meantime, I'll beg you to believe that my fine lady is making what she can. It's true she will have to end by swallowing the pill – but by then half the trees will have gone.'

'But how can she find anyone to buy, if she hasn't the right to sell?'

'Oh, you're very innocent still! When things are going for nothing, there's always someone to buy.'

'Any bailiff might prevent it.'

'The bailiff is in collusion with the creditors' agent, who has taken up his abode here;' he stopped and whispered in my ear: 'he sleeps with her, since you must know everything.'

'Monsieur Floche's books and papers?' I asked, without appearing disturbed by his last remark.

'There is shortly to be a sale of the library and furniture – or, to be more accurate – an execution. Fortunately no one here suspects the value of some of the books – or they would have disappeared long ago.'

'But suppose some rascal turned up . . .'

'No fear; the seals have been affixed; they won't be removed till the inventory has to be made.'

'And what does the Baronne say to it all?'

'She has no idea what is going on; her food is taken to her in her room; she doesn't even know her daughter is here.'

'You haven't mentioned the Baron.'

'He died three weeks ago in a nursing home at Caen just after we had managed to get him into it.'

We had reached Pont-l'Évêque. A priest came to meet Abbé Santal, who took leave of me, after having told me of an hotel and a livery stable.

The carriage I hired next day dropped me at the entrance to the park; it was settled the man should come and pick me up in a couple of hours' time, after the horses had rested in a neighbouring farm stables.

I found the iron gates wide open; the road had been ploughed up by heavy carts. I was expecting the most frightful devastation, and it gave me a joyful surprise as I entered to find my old friend the 'peach-leaved beech' in full bud; I did not stop to reflect that it no doubt owed its life only to the inferior quality of its wood; as I went on my way, I saw that the finest trees had already fallen to the axe. Before advancing further into the park, I wanted to revisit the little lodge where I had discovered Isabelle's letter; but the broken lock was now supplemented by a padlock on the door (I learned afterwards that the woodcutters used the lodge to keep their tools and coats in). I turned my steps towards the château. The path I followed was straight and bordered on each side by low bushes; it did not come out at the front of the house but at the side offices and led to the kitchen, almost opposite to which was a small gate opening into the kitchen garden; I was still some way off it when I saw Gratien come out of the garden with a basket of vegetables; he saw me without at first recognizing me; I hailed him and he came up to me.

'Well, I never! Monsieur Lacase!' he exclaimed. 'We weren't expecting *you*, sir, at this time of day!'

He stood looking at me, wagging his head and not attempting to hide his vexation at my appearance; he added, however, more mildly:

'The boy will be pleased to see you, though.'

We had taken a few steps without speaking in the direction of the kitchen; he signed to me to wait for him while he went in to put down his basket.

'So you've come to see what's going on at La Quartfourche,' said he, more civilly, as he came back.

'And it seems things are not going very well?'

I looked at him; his chin was trembling; he stood without answering; then, abruptly seizing me by the arm, he dragged me up to the lawn in front of the house. There lay the dead body of a monster oak, underneath which I remembered having taken shelter in the autumn. It had been stripped of its branches before being felled and now they were piled all round it in heaps of logs and bundles of faggots. . . .

'Do you know how much a tree like that is worth?' said he. 'Twelve *pistoles*! And do you know what they've paid for it? For that and the others too. . . . Five francs!'

I did not know that in that part of the world a ten-franc piece was called a *pistole*; but it was not the moment for explanations. Gratien went on with a choking voice. I turned to look at his face; he was wiping away tears or sweat with the back of his hand:

'Oh, the ruffians!' he exclaimed, clenching his fists, 'the ruffians! When I hear their hatchets and their axes I'm like to go mad, Sir; the blows fall on my own head; I want to call out "Help! Murder!" I want to use a hatchet to them myself. I want to kill them! I spent half the day yesterday trying not to hear their noise in the cellar; it wasn't so loud there. At first it amused the boy yonder to watch the woodcutters at their work; when the tree was ready to fall, they called him to pull the string; but when the ruffians brought their felling nearer the house, he didn't think it so funny. "Oh, not that one!" he says, "not this one!" "My poor lad!" says I, "don't worry about this or that — they won't leave you a single one." I've told him straight he won't be able to stay on at La Quartfourche; but he's too young yet; he can't get it into his head that none of it's his any longer. If only we could be kept on at the little farm; I'd have him to live with us gladly, you may be sure; but it'll be bought by the Lord knows who, and what manner of rascal will be put in instead of us? ... Look you, Sir, I'm not so very old yet, but I'd liefer have died than see what I've seen.'

'Who is living in the château now?'

'Don't ask me! The boy, he eats with us in the kitchen. It's better so. Madame la Baronne can't leave her room. Lucky for her, poor lady! ... Delphine takes her her meals — by the backstairs — so as not to come across certain people we won't mention. They have someone else to wait on them, but we don't speak.'

'Isn't there going to be a sale of the furniture soon?'

'When that comes we shall try and get Madame la Baronne to the farm — until that's put up for sale too with the château.'

'And Made ... and her daughter?' I asked hesitatingly, for I was at a loss what to call her.

'I don't care where she goes, as long as it isn't near us. To think that all this has happened along of her.'

I understood then – anger so deep and so grave trembled in his voice – that this man might have been capable of committing a crime in defence of his masters' honour.

'Is she in the house now?'

'It's likely she's walking in the park. She doesn't seem to feel it; she watches the woodcutters at work; some days she even talks to them, she's so lost to shame! But when it rains she doesn't leave her room – see, up there, the corner one! She stands close to the window and looks out at the garden. If her man weren't at Lisieux just now, I shouldn't be about as I am. Ah! Monsieur Lacase, they're fine gentry, you may take my word for it! If my poor old masters came back and saw what's going on in their home, they'd soon want to go back to the place they came from!'

'Is Casimir anywhere about?'

'I think he's in the park too. Shall I go and call him for you?'

'No; I shall easily find him. Good-bye for the present. I shall see Delphine and you again no doubt before I leave.'

The havoc caused by the woodcutters seemed still more cruel at this time of year when everything was awakening to new life. Young shoots were already swelling in the milder air; already buds were bursting and every severed branch was weeping tears of sap. I walked on slowly, the stricken landscape moving me not so much to sadness as to intenser consciousness; and perhaps the smell of vegetation that exhaled so powerfully from dying tree and travailing earth went a little to my head like wine. I was hardly sensible of the contrast between the corpses that strewed the ground and the reawakening spring; the park lay more open thus to the light that bathed both death and life alike in a golden glory; but yet the tragic song of the blows that rang through the distance, filling the air with a funereal solemnity, kept secret time to the happy beatings of my heart; and the old love-letter I had brought with me, though I had sworn to myself not to use it, burnt my breast as from time to time I pressed it to my heart. Nothing shall stand in my way today, I said to myself, and I smiled to myself, and I smiled to feel my step grow quicker at the mere thought of Isabelle; my will was in abeyance; it was a hidden power within that drove me. How strange it was that, by some over-abundance of life in me, the note of savage violence which all this devastation added to the beauty of the landscape only intensified my pleasure in it; how strange that the Abbé's calumnies had so little succeeded in detaching me from Isabelle, and that all I heard about her only gave a secret relish to the keenness of my desire. ... What was it that kept her in this spot which was so peopled with hideous memories? The sale of La Quartfourche could bring her – would leave her nothing. Why had she not fled from it? And I dreamed of bearing her off that very evening in my carriage; I walked more hurriedly – I was almost running, indeed, when suddenly, there in the distance before me, I caught sight of her. There was no doubt about it. It was she, in mourning and bareheaded, sitting on the trunk of a felled tree which had fallen across the path. My heart was beating so fast that I had to stop for a moment or two; then I went up to her slowly – a calm, indifferent gentleman taking an evening stroll.

'Excuse me, Madame ... can you tell me whether this is La Quartfourche?'

Beside her on the tree-trunk was a little work-basket full of reels, sewing materials and pieces of *crêpe*, some rolled up in bundles, others lying loose; she was employed in arranging one or two of these scraps on a dowdy little felt hat, which she was holding in her hand; a green ribbon she had no doubt just torn from it was lying on the ground. She was wearing a very short black cloth cape over her shoulders, and when she raised her head, I noticed the common little clasp at the neck. She had no doubt seen me in the distance, for she did not seem surprised by my voice.

'Have you come about buying the place?' she said, and my heart beat as I recognized her voice. How beautiful I thought her uncovered brow!

'Oh, simply to look at it. The park gates were open and I saw there were people about inside. But perhaps it was indiscreet of me to come in?'

'Anybody who likes may come in now!' She heaved a deep sigh, but returned again to her work as if we could have nothing more to say to one another.

I did not know how to continue the conversation: it was an opportunity which would probably never offer itself again – which would certainly be decisive; and yet I did not feel that the moment had come to precipitate matters; in my anxiety to be cautious, therefore, my heart and head filled with hopes and questions I did not as yet dare formulate, I remained speechless, poking with the end of my stick at some little chips of wood on the ground, so embarrassed, so awkward, and so impertinent withal, that at last she raised her eyes, stared at me and was, I thought, going to burst out laughing; but – no doubt because in those days I wore a soft hat and my hair long and did not seem to have any very urgent occupation – all she said was:

'Are you an artist?'

'Unfortunately not,' I answered, smiling; 'but that doesn't prevent me from appreciating poetry.' And though I did not as yet dare to look at her, I felt her eyes resting on me. Our hypocritical commonplaces were odious and I hate having to repeat them.

'How beautiful the park is!' I went on.

She seemed to wish for nothing better than to talk, and

was only embarrassed, like myself, by the difficulty of knowing how to start the conversation, for she exclaimed at once that unfortunately at this time of year the park was still shivering with cold and barely awakened out of its winter sleep, and that it was impossible to judge of what it was like in autumn – 'at least of what it used to be like,' she corrected herself; 'for what will be left of it, when the woodcutters have finished their dreadful work? . . .'

'Couldn't they be prevented?' I cried.

'Prevented!' she repeated ironically, and shrugged her shoulders; and I thought she was showing me her shabby felt hat to bear witness to her destitution, but she merely picked it up in order to put it on (she wore it tipped back so as to leave her forehead bare); then she began to arrange her pieces of *crêpe* as if she were getting ready to go. I stooped down, picked up the green ribbon at her feet and handed it to her.

'What is the use of it now?' she said, without taking it. 'You see I am in mourning.'

I immediately said how sorry I had been to hear of Monsieur and Madame Floche's death and recently too of the Baron's; and as she expressed astonishment at my having known her family, I told her I had spent ten days with them last October.

'Then why did you pretend not to know where you were just now?' she rejoined abruptly.

'I had to find an excuse for speaking to you.'

Then, without as yet showing my hand too openly, I began to tell her of the passionate curiosity which had kept me at La Quartfourche day after day in the hopes of meeting her and (I did not mention the night on which I had watched her so indiscreetly) of my regret at having to go back to Paris without having seen her.

'What gave you such a desire to know me?'

She no longer made as though to go. I had dragged up
a big bundle of wood on which I sat down close to her and
facing her; I was lower than she was and had to look up in
order to see her face; she was childishly busied in rolling
up her *crêpe* ribbons into little balls and I could not catch
her eyes. I spoke of her miniature and of my anxiety to
know what had become of the picture I had fallen in love
with; but she could not tell me.

'I suppose it will be found when the seals are removed
... and it will be put up to auction with the rest,' she added,
with a hard laugh that was painful to hear. 'You will
be able to get it for a few pence, if you still have a fancy for
it.'

I protested I was grieved to see she did not take me
seriously; that it was only their expression that was sudden,
but that these feelings had occupied me for a long time past;
she remained impassive, however – resolved, apparently, to
have nothing more to do with me. Time was pressing. But
had I not in my possession something that would force her
defences? The letter – the ardent letter lay quivering in my
hand. I had prepared some story or other of an old connexion between my family and the Gonfrevilles, thinking it
might induce her to speak; but at that moment I felt the
absurdity of such a falsehood and began quite simply to
relate by what mysterious chance the letter – I held it out to
her – had fallen into my hands.

'Ah! I implore you,' I cried, 'do not tear it up! Give it
back to me ...'

She had turned deadly pale and kept the letter open on
her knees for a few moments without reading it; with
vaguely staring eyes and fluttering eyelids, she murmured:

'Forgotten it! How could I have forgotten it?'

'You must have thought it had reached him, that he had
fetched it. ...'

She was not listening to me. I made a motion to take the letter back again, but she misunderstood it:

'Leave me!' she cried, pushing my hand away roughly. She rose and tried to go. On my knees before her, I held her back.

'Do not be afraid,' I cried; 'can't you see I wish you no harm?'

And as she sat down again, or rather sank down powerless, I begged her not to be angry with me if chance had chosen me to be her involuntary confidant, and implored her to complete a confidence which I swore not to betray; oh! would she not speak to me now as to a true friend who knew nothing but what she herself had told me?

The tears I shed as I spoke were more convincing perhaps than my words.

'Alas!' I went on, 'I know what a melancholy fate deprived you of your lover that very evening. ... But how did you learn your loss? What did you think that night as you were waiting for him, prepared to fly? What did you do when you saw he was not coming?'

'Since you know everything,' said she in a heartbroken voice, 'you must know that there was no question of my expecting him, once I had forewarned Gratien.'

The dreadful truth came upon me with such a flash of intuition that the next words broke from me like a cry:

'What! it was *you* who had him killed!'

Dropping the letter, the work-basket and all its contents on to the ground, she buried her face in her hands and began to sob desperately. I leant towards her and tried to take one of her hands in mine.

'No! You are ungrateful – brutal!'

My rash exclamation had cut short her confidences and hardened her heart against me; I still remained, however, sitting in front of her, firmly resolved not to leave her till she had explained herself more fully. Her sobs at last subsided; I persuaded her gently that now she had said so much, she could not possibly keep silent as to the rest, but that a sincere confession would not make me think ill of her, and nothing she could say would grieve me more than a refusal to speak. With her elbows on her knees, and her clasped hands hiding her face, this is what she told me:

She had written the letter in a state of passionate excitement during the watches of the night preceding the one she had fixed on for her flight; the next morning she had taken it to the lodge and slipped it into the hiding-place which Blaise de Gonfreville knew of and from which she counted on his shortly taking it. But as soon as she got back to the château, as soon as she found herself again in the room she had wished to leave for ever, she had been overcome by a dreadful, unspeakable misgiving – fear of the unknown liberty she had so savagely desired, fear of the lover she still longed for, and of herself, and of what she dared not venture. Yes, she had made the resolve; yes, she had repressed her scruples, swallowed her shame, but now that nothing held her back, now that the door stood open for her flight, her heart suddenly failed her. The idea of flight became odious to her – intolerable; she rushed to tell Gratien that the Vicomte de Gonfreville had planned to carry her off that very night, that he would be found towards evening loitering in the neighbourhood of the lodge gates and that he must be prevented from coming further.

I expressed astonishment that she had not simply gone herself to fetch back her letter and replaced it by another in which she might have dissuaded her lover from the mad scheme. But she evaded all the questions I put her and kept repeating with tears that she knew I should not be able to understand her, that she could not explain herself better, but that at the time she had felt as little able to repulse her lover as to follow him, that fear had paralysed her to such an extent that she was physically incapable of returning to the lodge; that, besides, at that time of day the parents she dreaded so were watching her, which was really the reason she had been obliged to have recourse to Gratien.

'Could I imagine he would take my wild words so seriously? I thought he would merely keep him off. . . . An hour later, I was startled by hearing a gunshot in the direction of the gates; but my thoughts recoiled from such a horrible supposition and I refused to contemplate it; on the contrary, since I had spoken to Gratien, I felt almost joyful, with a load taken off my heart and mind. . . . But when night came, when the hour that should have been that of my flight drew near, ah! in spite of myself, I began to feel expectant, I began to feel hopeful once more; a kind of confidence, which yet I knew was unfounded, mingled with my despair; I could not realize that the cowardice, the weakness of a moment had shattered my long dream at one blow; I was still not awake; yes, it was still in a dream that I went down into the garden, ears and eyes on the watch for every noise and every shadow; I waited – I waited on and on . . .'

She began to sob again:

'No, I was not waiting for anything any more,' she went on; 'I tried to deceive myself, and out of pity for my own self I acted the part of someone waiting and expecting. I had sat down by the lawn, on the lowest step of the perron; my heart too dry to shed a tear thinking of nothing, knowing neither who I was, nor where I was, nor what I had come there to do. The moon, which had been shining on the grass, disappeared, then an icy shudder seized me; I wished it could have frozen me to death. Next day, I fell seriously ill and the doctor who was called in informed my mother of my pregnancy.'

She stopped for a few moments.

'You know now what you wanted to know. If I were to go on with my story, it would be that of another woman, and you would not recognize the Isabelle of the locket.'

As it was, I could hardly recognize the Isabelle my imagination had fallen in love with. Her tale, it is true, was interlarded with interjections; she recriminated against fate; she lamented that in this world poetry and sentiment are always in the wrong; but it grieved me not to hear in her melodious voice any of the warm harmonics of the heart. Not a word of regret for anyone but herself! What! I thought, is *that* the only way she can love? . . .

I began to pick up the small objects that had fallen out of her overturned work-basket. I had no further desire to question her; I suddenly lost all curiosity as to her person and her life and stood before her like a child with a toy he has broken in order to discover its mystery; and even the physical attraction that was still hers no longer stirred in me the slightest trouble of the senses − not even the voluptuous droop of her eyelids which a moment before had made me tremble. We spoke of her want of means; and as I asked her what she intended to do ı

'I shall try to give lessons,' she replied; 'piano or singing lessons. I have a very good technique.'

'Ah! You sing?'

'Yes, and play. I once worked very hard at it. I was a pupil of Thalberg's . . . I am very fond of poetry too.'

And as I found nothing to say:

'I am sure you know some by heart! Won't you repeat me something?'

Distaste − disgust − for this trivial talk about poetry finally drove love from my heart! I rose to take my leave.

'Oh, are you going already?'

'I am sorry, but you must see yourself that it is better for me to leave you now. Try to imagine that last autumn, when I was staying with your people, the drowsy air of La Quartfourche lulled me to sleep, that I fell in love with a dream, and that I have just woken up. Good-bye.'

A little limping form appeared at the further end of the path.

'There is Casimir, I think. He will be glad to see me.'

'He is coming here. Wait for him.'

The boy came along in little hops; he was carrying a rake on his shoulder.

'If you will allow me, I will go to meet him. It might make him feel shy to see me with you. Excuse me. . . .' And hurrying over my farewells as awkwardly as I well could, I bowed respectfully and left her.

I never saw Isabelle de Saint-Auréol again and heard nothing more of her. Yes, once though. When I returned to La Quartfourche the following autumn, Gratien told me that just before the sale of the furniture she had been deserted by the estate-agent and had gone off with a coachman.

'You see, Monsieur Lacase,' he added sagaciously, 'she never could live alone; she always had to have a man of some sort.'

The La Quartfourche library was sold in the middle of the summer. In spite of my instructions, I was given no notice; and I think the Caen bookseller who was in charge of the sale was far from anxious to have me or any other serious connoisseur present. I learnt later on with amazement and indignation that the famous Bible had been sold for 70 francs to a second-hand bookseller in the neighbourhood, and re-sold immediately afterwards for 300 francs – I could never find out to whom. As for the seventeenth-century MSS, they were not even mentioned in the catalogue and were knocked down as waste-paper.

I should have. liked at any rate to have attended the sale of the furniture, for I had intended to buy a few small objects in memory of the Floches; but I was notified too late and arrived at Pont-l'Évêque only in time to be present at the sale of the house property and farms. La Quartfourche was knocked down for a trifling sum to the estate-agent Moser-Schmidt, who was on the point of turning the park into grass-land, when an American client bought it; I don't exactly know why, for he never returned to the country and leaves the park and château in the condition you saw.

As in those days I was far from well off, I meant to attend the sale merely as a spectator, but I had been to see Casimir that morning, and as I listened to the bidding, I was filled with such compunction at the thought of the poor little fellow's plight, that I suddenly resolved to settle him on the farm that Gratien had told me he wanted to occupy. You didn't know that it was my property? I ran up the bidding almost before I was aware of it; it was folly; but the poor child's melancholy pleasure more than recompensed me.

I spent the Easter holidays and the following summer holidays in the little farmhouse with Gratien and Casimir. Old Madame de Saint-Auréol was still living; we had managed somehow or other to give her the best room; she was now in her dotage, but able to recognize me and remember my name more or less:

'How kind of you, Monsieur de La Case! How kind of you!' she kept repeating, when she first saw me again. For she flattered herself that I had come back solely to visit her.

'They are making alterations up at the château. It will be very fine!' she said to me confidentially, by way of explaining to me – or to herself – her change of circumstances.

The day the furniture was put up for sale, she had been rolled out of the drawing-room on to the perron steps in

her big arm-chair; the bailiff had been introduced as a cele-
brated architect who had come from Paris on purpose to
supervise the building alterations; then Gratien, Casimir
and Delphine had carried her to the room in the farmhouse
which she had never left again, though she lingered on for
another three years.

It was during those first summer holidays, which I spent
on my farm, that I made the acquaintance of the B's, whose
eldest daughter I afterwards married. La R., which came
to us after the death of my parents-in-law, is not, as you saw,.
very far from La Quartfourche; two or three times a year
I go over and have a talk with Gratien and Casimir. They
cultivate their farm very well and pay their small rent
regularly. That was where I went this afternoon when I
left you.

The night was far advanced by the time Gérard had
finished telling us his story. But it was nevertheless that
same night that Jammes wrote his fourth elegy before
going to sleep – the one that begins: '*You asked me to
write an elegy on the deserted park, where the great
gales . . .*'